Isle of

Hogs

A Dragon Spawn Novella
(Follows Book Three or Four)

By Dawn Ross
© 2023

"Well, I was never much good at games. Always hated to lose."
– John Silver – Treasure Planet

Isle of Hogs

A Dragon Spawn Novella
(Follows Book Three or Four)

by Dawn Ross

Cover
The ship art was created by Nikolay Mossolaynen and purchased under the standard license agreement through 123rf.com in 2023. The skull art was created by Ilya Lukichev and also purchased under the standard license agreement through 123rf.com in 2023. The starry background is a public domain image from NASA. All the images were combined to create the cover by germancreative on fiverr.com.

Special Thanks

I'd like to extend a special thanks to all the beta readers and editors who helped me make this novel shine. And additional thanks to my final editor, Grace Bridges, who has been instrumental in helping me with content and line edits as well as with pointing out opportunities for story improvement.

Reviews for StarFire Dragons:

"A thoughtful novel that owes a debt to
Star Trek but works on its own terms."
—Kirkus Reviews

"A subtle space opera that explores the ethical
conundrums of intergalactic relations with main
characters who are worth rooting for."
—Becca Saffier, *Reedsy Discovery*

"Fans of epic sci-fi that look for realistic characters and complex
yet believable settings will find *Starfire Dragons*
a powerful introductory story that promises more, yet
nicely concludes its immediate dilemmas."
—D. Donovan, Senior Reviewer, *Midwest Book Review*

Isle of Hogs

A Dragon Spawn Novella
by Dawn Ross

1
Night Raid

3791:156:03:15. Year 3791, day 156, 03:15 hours, Prontaean time as per the last sync.

Two distant moons glowed like fingerprints on a biometric scanner. Their light barely outshone the swath of stars in the sky. Far from their gravitational pull, the sea was relatively calm. The stars glittered like unobtainable jewels in the small, wind-formed waves.

Captain Pak scratched his stubbly chin. He took in the warm, salty air, hating how much thicker it was by the shore. Something buzzed and landed on his ear, so he swatted it. The damn thing was big enough to make his hand smart, but the crunch and squish named it dead.

Mire sloshed and leaves rustled. Pak switched his cybernetic eye to thermal view. Three human-sized blobs broke through the brush on the opposite bank. Barty and Bull dumped their prisoner into the raft tethered to a mangrove root, then tottered in after. The water plopped and gurgled as they rowed.

About time. Pak stepped off the submarine gangplank. The ground here was spongy but more solid than the rest. Frogs and other night animals hopped or flitted away. One squished under his boot with a squeal and squelch.

The raft reached his side of the shore. Barty and Bull exited with their prisoner. Pak switched to night vision, turning everything into a monochrome slime color. All three wore raggedy clothes, though his men also wore old chest plates constructed with a composite material. Night optical devices covered their eyes while bandanas hid their balding heads and the bottom half of their faces. Telling them apart was easy. Bull was wide and Barty was all reeds and twigs.

The semi-conscious young man hanging by his arms between them was thinner. Pak grabbed his chin and looked him over. The bloody nose and busted lip glistened black in the dark, but the damage was minimal. The youth's bony jaw was firm. Good, but hardly a feature that'd fetch a decent price in the slave markets.

"Is this the best you could do?" Pak asked.

"Sorry, Cap," Barty replied in his low, raspy voice. "Not much pickins here. The goats have more meat on them than these folk."

Pak harrumphed. He felt the boy's arms and tapped his chest. *Not much meat indeed.* "Stand him up."

Barty and Bull hefted him to his feet. His head bobbled and he moaned, but he didn't regain full consciousness.

"He fight you?" Pak asked.

"Yep. Throws quite a punch," Bull replied.

"I s'pose he'll do." Pak stepped back and waved his hand. "Get him inside. Let the doc take a look at him."

Barty hauled the prisoner by his shoulders while Bull grabbed him by the shirt collar. The young man woke with a yelp. He kicked and Barty nearly stumbled off the gangplank. Bull decked him, silencing him once more.

Pak cursed. "Careful! I don't wanna have to get another. We spent enough time on this shitty island."

Although someone in better shape than this scrawny farmer would fetch a higher price in the city, Pak's patron cared more about the subjects' health. If Bull broke something the doc couldn't fix, they'd have to chop him up and feed him to the sharks.

He had eighteen people in the hold of his main ship. Men, women, young, middle-aged—all peasants. This skinny kid made nineteen. He needed just one more, then he could get the hell away from this forsaken island.

The submarine's top hatch hissed open. Light spilled out but didn't touch the depths of the surrounding jungle nor penetrate the inlet's black waters. It reflected off a pair of eyes in the woods, but only for a moment as the unknown animal scurried off.

"Cap," Barty said after Bull took the boy inside. "We saw a girl that'd make a nice addition. Her farm ain't too far off. Maybe we got time to get her tonight."

Pak chewed his lip. Getting back to his ship and sleeping in a proper bed rather than in the bunk down below had its appeal. Plus, he had his good stash there. All he had here was a cheap, sharp tequila that burned long after being swallowed.

He accessed his cranial implant. Only eighty-six minutes until the sun rose. "These farm folk get up early. Can't chance being seen."

Barty shrugged. He flicked a bug off his arm before heading back to the sub. Pak swatted away a swarm of insects buzzing in his face and spit. He hated this hellish jungle, but the competition and danger involved in abduction forced them into ass-end places like this.

Just one more damn night on this tin can and they'd be done. From the generosity his patron had shown before, two more runs would give him enough to buy a new ship. Slavers didn't pay half as well, certainly not for scrawny stock like the ones here. But his patron didn't plan on selling them as slaves.

Rats. That's what they'd be. Good old-fashioned lab rats.

2
Isle of Hogs

The sharp, burning odor wafting from the stomach-turning pile of pig shit melded with misery. Terkeshi wrinkled his nose but endured. He wiped the sweat from his forehead with the crook of his arm. A half-dozen flies buzzed away at the last moment, but quickly returned.

The ones landing on the left of his scarred face created a ghosted sensation, something akin to hairs standing on end. He involuntarily touched his brow, tracing his fingers over the bumpy lizard-like skin that'd melted and scarred over his cheek and missing eye. He'd never get used to not being able to see from that side.

It was unlikely he'd ever get a replacement eye. Nor could he afford to have the scarring removed. The burn marks left by the damaged nanite mask would probably stay forever. The islanders knew him as Terk but had no idea he'd once been Prince Terkeshi Mizuki. He was too ugly now to be anything other than a lowly peasant.

With a grunt, he scraped the last load of manure-caked straw onto his pitchfork and heaved it over the side of the pigpen and into the wheelbarrow. Pigs only a little bigger than Baba Airi's dog milled about with disgruntled snorts. One interfered by nosing at his rubber boots.

"Get back, stupid." He nudged the surly animal aside.

The pig squealed in protest but trotted away to see what his buddies were up to. Terk propped his pitchfork against a post, then hopped over the fence. His boots pounded the dry dirt with a puff of dust. He wiped his sweaty palms down his manure-colored pants, hating the loose, coarse material and missing his form-fitting, temperature-regulating uniform.

He peered at the oppressive blue sky. Not a single cloud marred it, which meant it would be another blistering day. He groaned and cursed under his breath.

The strangeness of turning from a warrior prince to a peasant farmer had long since worn off. Wrestling livestock and scooping their crap had replaced his daily martial practices. Instead of living on a spaceship where the air recyclers kept odors at bay, he endured the constant smell of animals and dirt. And while the air on the ship was generally moderate, the weather here was always hot with an occasional side of muggy.

This was his life now, and he hated it.

When he'd first approached this planet from space, he admired how it sparkled like a beautiful sapphire against a backdrop of stars. Every hour he advanced brought its dazzling details into focus. Not even the specks of rich brown land masses marred the beauty of the planet's crystalline oceans.

He still remembered how his hope and yearning had swelled. This place offered freedom from the violence of his domineering father. His little brother Jori and his mentor Sensei Jeruko were dead, but he'd tried not to think about them. Finding his mother was supposed to help him start anew.

Things hadn't gone as expected. Although she lived on this island, it wasn't safe to visit her. Father thought he'd died, and he wanted to keep it that way. Not to mention the personal danger he'd be in if others saw him with his mother and put two and two together.

He was stuck in anonymity on this pitiful farm surrounded by a sunbaked jungle. He resented it, but whenever he tried to blame others, like his father, it rounded back to him. This was his own doing. He'd done this to himself.

If he could do it again knowing what would be in store for him… Well, he'd still choose the stinky livestock and this dirty little farm over his asshole father.

"Terk!" a high-pitched voice sounded from the other side of the barn. It wasn't a desperate yell, but Baba Airi wouldn't call for him unless she needed help.

Terk ran over the hard dirt and through the short brown grass. Rounding the corner of the dilapidated structure, he found the old woman doubled over and panting. Beside her lay an overturned wheelbarrow of food waste and foraged grub.

"Baba! What are you doing? I told you I'd take care of that."

She waved him off. "I know. I know. I just didn't want to leave you with all the hard work."

"Don't be ridiculous. I can handle it."

He almost laughed at the irony. When Washi and Michio, his old personal guards who'd been exiled to this island by his father, had sent him here, he'd refused to do anything. He lay in bed all day while Baba Airi did everything. It was her damn farm, after all.

The more the old woman worked, the more he'd grown to admire her. Eventually, his pride shifted. Since she struggled day in and day out and still cooked him an evening meal, the least he could do was get his pathetic ass out of bed and help.

He hated the work, but not her. Baba Airi had a personality as cheerful as the birds in the forest. Her attitude extended to everything she did and everyone she was around, including the animals.

Terk gave her a mock-stern look as he righted the wheelbarrow and tossed the slop back inside. She returned it with a half-smile, her ice-blue eyes twinkling like they always did. Although she wore her grey hair pulled back into a tail, wisps of it stuck out from her head. Her skin was darker than his and wrinkled worse than dried fruit. As old as she was, she still had a sharp mind—and a warm heart to match.

Everyone called her baba even though she wasn't anyone's grandmother. With no children of her own, she'd taken in many others over the years. His arrival had come in her greatest time of need. Her health was failing, but she didn't give up. The animals, and the people they helped nourish, still needed her.

She patted his back. "You're a good, strong boy. I'll tend to the chickens instead."

Terk shook his head. So much work for just a few beasts. "Why do you raise real animals? Isn't it cheaper and faster to grow the meat in vats?"

"If you have the money to buy the machines and the know-how to do it. We don't have those things here."

"Hmm." As difficult as his previous life had been, he hadn't realized how much he'd taken for granted. His father had always been hard on him—sometimes too hard—but at least his basic needs were met.

Terk left her to the chickens and headed back to the pigpen where the little beasts had already trampled a mud puddle by the waterspouts. They scrambled to the gate when he arrived. Since food had arrived, they followed him to the trough rather than try to escape. He dumped the slop in, wincing at the twinge caused by the burn scars on his right palm. The way they pulled at his skin made it more difficult to wield a practice weapon—and sometimes a pitchfork too.

I'm hardly good enough to be a farmer now.

He swallowed down the bitterness and went back to work. Halfway through laying fresh straw, a grinding rumble sounded from over the hill. Terk ambled toward the road to meet the visitor.

Unlike the slow grating of a tractor, the ATV rolled in like a military assault vehicle. The man at the wheel drove it like one as well. A trail of dirt spewed out from the back tires and it fishtailed on the gravel.

Terk planted his hands on his hips and waited. The vehicle arrived with a hard brake. Dust plumed, then settled. The man who stepped out of the open cockpit resembled the deceased Sensei Jeruko. Terk's heart wrenched. Washi had the same sturdy and self-assured build, ebony hair—though his had no silver in it—and similar eyes. Except for the goatee sparsely concealing a dimpled chin, he was a younger replica.

His clothes differed from when he'd served the emperor. Back on the warship, he'd worn an all-black uniform embedded with top-grade armor. Here, his military garb was brown with green trim, and scuffed and patched.

"Have you seen Xiaobo?" Washi asked.

Terk scoffed. "He wouldn't come here. He knows I hate him."

"Maybe he stopped by and made trouble. You defended yourself and took it too far. Killed him."

Terk fumed but also shrank under accusation. He'd beaten Xiaobo up before—even breaking a rib that could've caused internal damage—but that chima had started it. Still, he wouldn't kill someone just because he didn't like them. Then again, his actions had gotten a lot of good people killed. "As much as I would love to give him another ass-kicking, I haven't seen him."

Washi held eye contact for a few tense moments, then shrugged. "Only making sure."

Terk kept back a heated reply. When he'd been the son of the notorious Dragon Emperor, Washi had treated him with respect. Now he looked at him with barely contained contempt.

Washi blamed him for the death of his father. Sensei Jeruko had been much like a father to Terk, too. He'd never do anything to put him in danger, but that was what had happened. He resented the new way Washi regarded him, but his guilt was stronger.

"Well, he's the third from this village to go missing this week," Washi continued. "I'm guessing slavers are snatching them up."

Terk twisted his mouth at the thought of low-life slavers. His anger mingled with worry for the decent people he'd met here. "Why would they come here? Surely there are better targets in the city."

"Cities have competition and it's easier to sneak about here."

Chusho. "Seems like a lot of work just to abduct a few isolated farmers." Terk eyed Baba Airi's meager field and the surrounding dry forest. The nearest homestead was a ten-minute walk away. "Let me help you find them. I have skills—"

Washi wagged his head. "I can't very well enlist you into guard detail without people wondering why I'm enlisting a fourteen-year-old."

"I'm almost fifteen," Terk muttered, chafing at how he'd once been on a path to be a great warrior but was now stuck cleaning up pig shit.

"They'll figure out who you are, and then where will you be? Dead, that's where."

Terk suppressed a groan. His old self would've argued the point, maybe even made a few derogatory remarks. No more. Besides, Washi was right. He couldn't risk certain people finding he was alive. Besides, arguing would only make Washi hate him more than he already did. Terk didn't want that. He wanted the old Washi, the serious yet understanding man who had guided his training and protected him from would-be assassins.

"How are the slavers getting here?" Terk asked. "Doesn't the island have defenses?"

He recalled his own flight to this island and how he'd needed to crash out at sea to keep from being detected. His little ship had a lifeboat in case of emergency planetary landings, but radar still would've triggered alarms and alerted the island's meager ground forces.

"My guess is they're coming in underwater."

Terk's brows rose. Why hadn't he thought of that? It would've been safer than convincing a fishing boat to take him to port and hope they didn't cut his throat along the way. "Why doesn't the island have underwater defenses?"

"With all the marine animals, sonar or any other detection device is more hassle than it's worth."

Makes sense. Dolphins, seals, and enormous fish filled the surrounding ocean. "So, what are you going to do?"

"For now, try to find out Xiaobo's last whereabouts and try to track him."

"Anything I can do to help?"

"Just be on the lookout. Go to the bell tower and call for the constable if you see something suspicious."

Terk crossed his arms. "I won't just run off. I'll stop those chimas and make them wish they'd taken up farming instead."

"Don't be stupid, boy." Washi's rebuke compelled Terk to look away. "By confronting them, you'll most likely step into a trap."

"If I run, they'll go after Baba Airi."

Washi barked a laugh that held no humor. "An old woman won't make a good slave. You try to handle it yourself with her around, they might hurt her. So the best way to keep her safe is to *alert the constable.*"

Terk bristled at having to follow the orders of someone he'd once commanded but didn't argue. "If we had an effective communication system, we could call him."

Washi shook his head. "Can't have communications on an island where people have been exiled."

"Not everyone was banished here."

"Rules are rules."

"Well, it's stupid."

Washi ignored him as though he wasn't worth the debate. After he left to finish his security rounds, Terk kicked a clod of dirt. It bounced over the parched land, creating little puffs of dust. He soured at how that dried clump had more value than he did nowadays.

3
Fallen Warrior

Terkeshi tightened the bolt then wriggled out from under the tractor, his back scraping the pebbly ground. The pesky black and white puppy that seldom left his side wagged his furry little tail and bowed into a frisky pose. Terk obliged him with a few playful smacks, almost smiling at how the pup tripped over his own feet.

He scratched the mutt's head and rose. After patting the dust from his pants and tattered tan shirt, he wiped the sweat from his brow. The grit scraped along his skin, probably leaving smudges of brown. With his work now done, he'd get cleaned up soon enough.

As if on cue, his ability to sense the lifeforce and emotions of others detected a familiar approach. Having to shift for his good eye to see Yuan waving annoyed him almost as much as seeing the guy himself.

Like the puppy, Yuan was a goofy-looking pest. He wore a lopsided smile under a crop of messy black hair. Even though he was a year older than Terk, the way he chatted about nonsense exposed his childishness.

When Terk had first met him and told him to leave him the hell alone, Yuan left with his head hanging. The idiot returned the next day with the same overenthusiastic friendliness. It didn't matter how many times Terk sent him away, he'd always come back.

He wasn't sure when it had begun, but Yuan was growing on him. It was hard to dislike someone so amiable and eager to lend a hand.

Terk put the tools in the toolbox. Yuan fell in beside him as they headed to the shed.

"You got everything done?"

"Yep." Terk ignored Yuan's approving smile. Not that long ago, the guy would arrive while he was still working. He'd resisted his help but was also secretly grateful for it. Now, he no longer needed it.

"Great! Let's go swimming. I might look for some crabs too. Maybe one of those giant ones. Then you and Baba can come to my place for dinner."

Terk didn't answer. Nor did he need to. Yuan chatted on, Terk half-listening as he set the tools on the workbench, then headed into the forest. A worn trail marked the way. So did a swarm of insects.

"Have you given him a name yet?" Yuan pointed at the lean pup with giant paws bounding ahead.

"Gaichu."

Yuan laughed. "So you'll just keep calling him *Pest*, then."

"That's what he is." Terk held back a smile. He'd initially called the pup Gaichu out of irritation. It'd become a term of endearment, but he dared not admit this out loud. Although he liked Yuan, the guy had a big mouth and Terk didn't like the idea of everyone knowing his sentiment for a stupid dog.

As Yuan chatted on, Terk reflected on the incident that'd changed his mind about the pup. When Gaichu was just a short fat thing that constantly pestered him, he'd kicked him out of agitation. The pup's whimpering cry had gnawed at his insides. Kicking a helpless creature was something his father would do, but he didn't want to be like that chima. So he made up with the little runt and they'd been companions ever since.

With Gaichu exploring up ahead, they followed the path until it met a churning stream. After a few more bends, the trees parted, revealing a clear pool fed by the island's mountains. It was large enough to swallow a farmstead but small enough to see the bit of blue on the male ducks on the other side. A broad strip of smooth rocks lined this part of the shore, providing plenty of room for the twenty or so young people who lounged there, chatting in between dips in the water.

The peaceful scene shattered at the squabble of two individuals.

"Leave me alone, you pimply toad!" Anxi shouted. Her freckles disappeared in the red of her face and her eyes flared like torches.

Lixin snickered but withdrew. His long arms would have swung across the ground like an ape's if he didn't also have long legs. At nineteen, he was the oldest and tallest here, but not as athletically built as Terk. Thin as many of these tree trunks, even Anxi had more muscle than that chima. It complemented her body well. Her face, however, left much to be desired. When she saw him, she smiled. It was pleasant enough, but he couldn't see past its frog-like wideness. Still, he admired her in a way.

Some weeks back, his sensing ability had detected her in a panic. He'd also felt Lixin's lust and knew exactly what was happening. By the time he arrived, Anxi stood over the bloodied guy with her fists at her side and a snarl worthy of a blackbeast. He'd laughed at Lixin's humiliation until Anxi faced him with a vow to do the same to him if he tried anything. Since that'd never been his intention, complying hadn't hurt his pride.

His musings fled when a younger girl waved at him with a different kind of smile on her face. He didn't recall her name. People from this island often had names derived from another branch of their ancestry, making them difficult for him to remember.

Xihuan. That was it. She liked him, but thirteen was too young for his tastes. Still, he returned the greeting, keeping it flat lest he give her the wrong impression.

"I don't know why," Anxi said, "but she has a crush on you."

Terk rolled his eyes, playing along. "Who doesn't?"

"Pigs don't count."

Terk smiled. Anxi had been wary of him at first. One day when he'd come here, she looked him up and down with her hands on her hips. *"What'd you do?"* she'd asked. *"Clean the pig pens by rolling around in their crap?"* He'd been too surprised to be upset, and she'd taken to teasing him ever since.

He took off his boots and entered the water with his dirty clothes on. Once up to his waist, he thrust his whole body in and swam. The cool water swept over him, washing away the day's grime.

Yuan and Gaichu joined in, but he went his own way, relishing both the water's resistance against his muscles and how it carried him across the mountain-fed pool. Swimming was the best thing about living on a planet.

At some point, Yuan and the pup got out—Yuan to socialize and Gaichu to explore. Terk swam on, getting lost in the rhythm of his breathing and strokes.

A fearful sensation crept into his senses. Lixin was harassing Yuan now. A glance revealed nothing physical, but he knew the bully well enough to know that would change if Yuan didn't give in to whatever his demands were.

Yuan had tried standing up for himself before, only to get beaten down. Terk sped up his swim with a desire to put that jerk in his place.

The force of the water attempted to hold him back as he waded out. Before he reached the shore, Gaichu decided he didn't like the situation either. The dumb mutt darted in front of Yuan and barked.

"You damned mongrel!" Lixin kicked and missed. With a curse, he threw a palm-sized rock, striking the dog in the leg.

Gaichu's yelping exploded Terk's fury. He stormed over, ready to snap the twig-framed guy in half. Lixin didn't notice. He picked up another stone.

A girl chopped it out of his hand and shoved him. "Leave him alone, coward!"

Lixin snarled at Anxi but backed up at Terk's approach.

"You're in trouble now," Anxi said. She stepped aside, letting Terk handle it from here.

Lixin faced Terk, spewing both fear and indignation. "Your stupid dog tried to bite me!"

Terk kept coming. Lixin's alarm spiked. He picked up another rock and threw it. Terk dodged but misjudged. It hit his shoulder, enraging him further. He charged.

Lixin scurried back, picking up and flinging more rocks. "Come on, one-eye." He laughed. "Come get me."

Something smacked Terk's temple. He growled. *Damn it!* He hadn't even seen that one coming. He picked up a stone of his own and pitched it. It bypassed Lixin, making the guy laugh harder.

Chusho! Having only one eye ruined his ability to aim. He was like a missile ready to explode but unable to hit a target.

Lixin yelped, sounding a little like Gaichu. Terk stopped, searching for the source. Anxi threw another rock, hitting that chima between the eyes. Terk rushed in at his disorientation and swung a fist. The impact to Lixin's side jarred Terk's scarred hand. *Damn it!* Despite several weeks of activity, these stupid handicaps still hindered him.

Lixin punched back. Terk blocked him with his forearm, then struck him in the jaw. Despite the resulting twinges from his old injury, Terk walloped him twice more. Lixin fell onto the rocks with a cry.

Exhilaration flushed through Terk's veins as he pummeled him. Lixin deserved it, and not just for what he did to Gaichu. Anxi wasn't the only girl he'd ever attacked and probably wouldn't be the last.

"Stop. I'm sorry," Lixin blubbered. "I'm sorry, alright? Stop."

Terk was beyond caring as a satisfying rage roared in his ears. The next punch split Lixin's lip open.

"Terk!" someone yelled.

Another person bellowed, "That's enough!"

Yuan's and Anxi's frantic voices intruded into Terk's emotions. What the hell were they upset about? Lixin had been nothing but a jerk to them too.

"Stop!" Yuan screamed. "You'll kill him!"

The words halted Terk's fist mid-strike. Washi had accused him of doing this very thing. An overwhelming shame doused his temper. Lixin's left eye was red. Blood pooled over his brow, splattered below his nose, and drizzled down his chin.

Terk's chest heaved as he attempted to get a hold of himself. As much as Lixin deserved a good ass-kicking, Terk could've beaten him to death. If he didn't learn to control himself, he'd be just like Father.

He rose and stepped back, his fists still clenched at his sides, and let Lixin crawl away. The guy's whimpering elicited sympathy from some others, which reignited Terk's anger. Now he was the bad guy, and everyone pitied that undeserving chima.

Terk stormed off. His emotions warred between hating himself and hating Lixin.

*****

The sun hovered just above the treetops. The heat of the day blew off a little at a time, brushing through the forest with a hush that soothed Terkeshi's nerves. He'd never cared for meditating, but it had become his new respite. The irony that he did more now than he'd done under Sensei Jeruko's tutelage wasn't lost on him. Losing his mentor had devastated him almost as much as losing his brother, but it also gave him a new appreciation for his teachings.

After one last deep inhale, Terk rose to his feet with a slow exhale. Gaichu wagged his tail and presented a stupidly adoring look.

The field between the forest line and the house remained deserted. Still no sign of Washi. Perhaps the search for Xiaobo had kept him from hearing about Lixin. He'd find out soon enough, though. Then Terk would get a lot more than a scolding.

He set aside his angst and retrieved the bow Baba Airi had given him. Her husband had constructed it some years ago, before an illness ended his life. She'd made the arrows herself, crafting perfectly straight shafts, deathly sharp points, and faultlessly symmetrical fletching.

The impulse to practice by throwing rocks instead came over him. If he'd been able to catch the projectiles and aim well enough to hit Lixin without causing serious damage, things never would've gone so far. But that skill wasn't as useful as this. Protecting Baba Airi's livestock from predators was part of his job now. And if slavers were on the island, he wanted to be prepared. A phaser would be better, but only certain soldiers could carry that kind of weapon.

With a determination to overcome his disabilities, Terk took a perpendicular stance with his feet shoulder-width apart. He eased back the bowstring with his left hand, ignoring the ache in his right, and aimed—or tried to. He had excellent vision, but distance played a factor when shooting primitive projectiles. Having one eye also limited his ability to gauge it. He had another aspect to consider— one that didn't apply when he'd trained using energy rifles. The wind's speed and direction meant he needed to adjust his aim.

A slow exhale released the last bit of tension in his shoulders. He loosed the arrow. The twang of the string was followed by the snap to his leather vambrace. Terk held his breath as the bolt sailed toward the target. Just when he was certain it would strike the bullseye, it didn't.

He tried several more times, getting lucky only once. He adjusted his aim a little more up and to the left. This arrow hit too far to the right. *Damn it!* He clenched his fists and wished the target had a face so he could punch it. If slavers ever attacked him, he might as well surrender.

Gritting his teeth, he retook his stance. As he pulled the bowstring, an ache blossomed in his right palm. He endured the burn that sent a tremble up his arm. When he fired, the bolt missed by a wide margin.

"Chusho!" He tossed the bow to the ground and roared. *Stupid scars!* No wonder Washi hadn't wanted his help. He was useless.

He shook his arm, hoping the pain would ebb, but only made it worse. This wouldn't be an issue if he was still a prince. Nano machines could heal him. Regrowth technology would give him a new eye. He'd be a warrior again.

A bitter laugh escaped his throat. Who was he kidding? He'd never been much of a warrior. His mounting failures had led him here where he barely cut it as a farmer.

He glowered at the target. The setting sun shaded it under the canopy of trees, but the bullseye still mocked him. He snatched up his bow and marched back to the hovel he now called home. Discouragement darkened his mood the way dusk dimmed the sky.

Prince or peasant, he was worthless.

4
Stepfather

The all-terrain vehicle jerked to a stop inside the garage. Washi Jeruko winced at how close he'd come to hitting the back wall. He'd been warned about his reckless driving but had let his temper blind him. If Father were still alive, he'd be disappointed. *Anger doesn't help anyone, son*, he used to say.

Although the man was right, Washi couldn't get rid of his cloudy mood. It had begun when the emperor killed Terkeshi's brother Jori, then ordered Washi and his brother Michio to be executed. If Father hadn't begged for their lives, they would've been executed.

Getting exiled to this island where he didn't have to put up with that madman anymore had almost been a relief. But then Terkeshi had shown up with news that Father was dead. The great Jin Jeruko, the best of the Jeruko family, was gone and it was all because of the emperor's sons.

And now Terkeshi was making more trouble. Washi's blood heated at what that boy had done. He was tempted him to knock some sense into him. If not for Anxi, he would've done just that. The girl argued on his behalf. Lixin always caused problems—him and Xiaobo both. But Washi didn't need yet another bully to contend with.

How can I get through to that boy? He remained in the ATV and took in several long breaths. The tingling in his nerves eased somewhat and logical thought returned.

Physical punishment wasn't the answer. No one, especially not someone as hotheaded as Terkeshi, ever responded well to violence. So what should he do? Send him somewhere else? No. That wouldn't work for two reasons. One, Terkeshi would find somebody else to clash with. Two, the boy was finally giving Baba Airi the help she needed—and doing a surprisingly good job at it.

He dropped his head against the back of the seat. What would Father do? He'd reason with him in that calm tone of his. He'd accept Terkeshi's excuses but offer better ways to handle it, all without demeaning him. His methods almost always worked, but Washi didn't think he could pull it off. The hard feelings he still harbored would probably cause him to lose his temper. Perhaps Michio would take care of it.

With that decided, he got out and slammed the vehicle door. Cooler air greeted him as dusk waned. He tried to enjoy it as he crossed the yard to his mother's house. Thanks to Father's desire to continue to care for her despite their separation and her exile, this place was a little bigger than most homesteads on the island. She received enough money to buy food from the locals, which meant she didn't have to tend her own fields or farm animals—though she took pride in her flower garden and chickens.

The screen door squealed open. The main one probably did as well, but the clanking in the kitchen drowned it out. The nutty, savory odor of the stir-fried vegetables mingled with the chicken simmering in chili sauce. His nostrils twitched and his mood lifted.

Entering the small house provided him with a full view of the room. The cooking area crowded next to the round dining table big enough to squeeze in five. A lace cloth covered its worn wood, but nothing hid the cracked and stained countertops or distressed cupboards in the kitchen.

Still, his mother had created a quaint space with her decorative luxuries. A beautiful silk painting hung on the far wall. Ornamental ceramic, bronze, and wooden knickknacks were displayed in out-of-the way spaces. And an ornate vase full of fresh flowers from her garden brought an elegance to the fancy but chipped dinnerware on the table.

"You're just in time! Sit down. I'm almost done." Despite her grey-streaked hair, her bright eyes gave her a younger look. She had a little paunch now, but the flared maroon dress she wore hid it.

He edged around her work area and sat at the table. Her smile remained as she finished up. She'd said she found happiness here, but he'd never believed it until being exiled himself. Between her flower garden and cooking, she took pride in this way of life.

He warmed at the thought. If only he could find that same peace.

"Jingyu will be here soon." Her smile dimpled her chin more but didn't detract from her elegant countenance.

Washi must've made a face because her mouth turned down. "No need to be a sourpuss. You have no reason to dislike him."

"He's not Father."

"No. *He's* my husband. Someone who's been by my side a lot longer than your father."

Washi clenched his teeth. His father had been a good man. It was the emperor who'd forced him to abandon her. "It just feels like a betrayal, especially now that he's dead."

Her face softened. "My relationship with him was over long before his passing." She stirred the food in the pan as it cooked. "And it was many years after that before I fell in love with Jingyu. He knew about him, you know."

Washi suppressed a grimace. He supposed he should be grateful he didn't have a stepbrother too.

"Let's just try to be a family again," she continued. "I realize it's not the same, but it's what we have."

He could almost hear her say, *I haven't had my family for so long.* That was what she'd said the first time he argued on Father's behalf—before he'd learned of his death. She had a point. When the emperor had sent her away, he and Michio were still children but old enough to remain under the tutelage of their father. They saw her every year or two, but it wasn't the same. She was practically a stranger to him, even now—which was probably another reason he resented Jingyu.

"Any luck finding the missing people?" she asked.

His mood dipped further. "No trace. If they arrived in an underwater craft, as I suspect, there are a million coves deep enough to hide in."

Her brows curled in. "But they're coming in on foot. Wouldn't they leave footprints?"

"The ground inland is too dry this time of year. And boars and other animals trample those trails."

She sighed. "I hope you find them."

Me too. Although exiled here, he'd been assigned to protect these people. Combine the vastness of the jungle with their lack of resources and his job was damn near impossible.

Michio's bell-like laughter from outside intruded on his thoughts. He ground his teeth, hating how well his little brother got along with Jingyu.

The two entered, both with cheeks red from their mirth. Michio had Washi's same build, hair and eye color, and goatee. The only noticeable differences were Michio's slenderer face and smaller eyes.

Jingyu looked nothing like any of them. His heavily lidded eyes made his sockets look like split star apple fruit. Everything about him was just as round—his face, his bald head, and his gut.

His mother welcomed them with a cheerful exclamation and merriness in her eyes.

"My love." Jingyu wrapped his arm around her waist and pecked her cheek, making Washi's nostrils flare.

When Jingyu turned a genuine smile Washi's way, it didn't dispel his irritation. He put on a friendly expression anyway. A raised eyebrow from Michio indicated it'd probably looked forced, so he tried again.

He rose to his feet, forcing a grin, and pulled out a chair. "Major."

Jingyu clapped him on the shoulder. "Come now. No need for that here."

At least he didn't add, *we're practically family*, like he had once before. That hadn't gone over well.

Jingyu joined him with an amiable mien. His smile remained, making his eyes narrower than usual.

"Any luck on your end?" Washi asked regarding the missing villagers.

Jingyu's expression fell. "I'm afraid not. I have people scrutinizing all the recordings from the motion cameras, but they don't cover the entire island." He folded his hands and leaned in. "I understand there was some trouble involving our new guest."

"Nothing serious," Washi replied.

"You sure? I heard otherwise."

Washi soured. Jingyu was well above his chain of command, so did he spy on him or was he just good at staying informed? Knowing his genuine interest in keeping the populace safe, it was probably the latter. Still, Washi hated how it made him feel singled out.

"Swollen bruises. That's all," Washi replied, hating to defend Terkeshi's temper. "And Lixin had it coming."

Jingyu knew Terkeshi was the emperor's son. He'd discovered him at the exiled empress' home when he'd stopped by to give Washi's mother a ride back to her place. The lady Amarante had begged him not to tell anyone her son was alive. Had she not been the dear friend of Jingyu's lover, the boy would've been turned over to the authorities.

Washi returned to the other subject. "We'd have better luck finding those people if we had more men assigned to the task."

Mother brought the last dish to the table and joined them. Jingyu put his hand over hers and smiled, then faced Washi. "If I could, I would. But it's not my call. And unfortunately, there is a greater threat we must prepare for."

"Greater than slavers taking our people?"

"Much. There's a mad dragon to contend with."

Washi's gut knotted. If the emperor's attention had fallen on this insignificant island, then maybe he knew about Terkeshi. This didn't just put the boy in danger, but *everyone*.

"He doesn't know his son is here," Jingyu said, guessing Washi's concern. "Our informants have confirmed that the emperor believes all his sons are dead."

"Why is he harassing us, then?"

"Paranoia. This island is full of his exiles. No matter what Lord Qing does, the emperor interprets it as a threat."

Great. Just what we need.

5
Abduction

Something moist stroked Terkeshi's face. His surging adrenaline spiked to the point of pain. The unknown source of wetness returned with an intense insistence. He frantically smacked it away. The replying yelp broke through his nightmare.

Terkeshi bolted upright and gasped for air. The surrounding darkness compounded his already racing heart. Panic suffocated him, gripping his chest like a salvage grappler. He wanted to lash out but didn't know who to fight. Where the hell was he, anyway?

A breeze swept by. A curtain whispered at an open window, revealing a dark starry sky. Wait, didn't he live on a ship? A pathetic whine broke through his terror. Since he saw only shadows, he reached out with his sensing ability.

The feel of Gaichu's lifeforce dampened his panic. He was in Baba Airi's home—his home now, too.

"Sorry, buddy," he whispered. Gaichu's tail thumped on the floor. "Come here." The pup scrambled over his blankets and bounded into his lap. Terk ran his hand down his soft fur. "Thank you for waking me."

The dream—or nightmare—flitted through his brain. He'd been strapped down as an articulated metal arm brought a needle closer to his eye. He'd tried to close it, but surgical implements held it open.

His heart thumped into a gallop once more as the nightmare flooded back. It wasn't really a nightmare, though—more like a horrifying memory.

Damn. He must've had this dream a hundred times now. It was almost always the same, but there'd been something different this time—something important. *What was it?* He ran his knuckles over his forehead, grasping at the fleeting images.

That's right. Someone else had screamed, interrupting his own shouts of terror as cyborgs with metallic skulls, robotic limbs, and machine bodies operated on him. A girl appeared. She'd punched and kicked at the two robots trying to restrain her. The strength of her fury sparked his memory. It was Anxi. What had she been doing in his nightmares?

He remembered being afraid for her. It was bad enough that they'd been turning him into a cyborg. He didn't want her to become one too. He'd raced toward her, but no matter how fast he ran, the distance remained the same.

Something else was weird about the dream. Somehow, he'd transitioned into Anxi and he was in a dark forest. Her captors had turned into men with cybernetic eyes. No. They wore night vision goggles as they dragged him—her—along. They'd seemed so real, more real than the other parts of his nightmare.

He shook his head, trying to get rid of the weirdness. It was over, but a lingering feeling prodded at him. He concentrated on it, intending to block it, but it sharpened. The terrified sensation filtered in from the outside, making him gasp.

His entire being shifted. One moment, he sat on a hard mattress. The next, he was in a dark forest with two cyborgs.

What in the holy hell!? The shock returned him to himself. A numbness crawled over him as he tried to process what'd just happened. The external fright shoved its way back into his senses and realization struck him. Somehow, he'd been inside Anxi's head again and she was in real trouble.

"Chusho!" He nudged Gaichu aside and threw off his blankets. "Baba!" He bounded over to the other side of the room. Gaichu barked in confusion. "Baba!"

The old woman bolted upright. She shied away from him in the darkness.

"Baba, it's me, Terk. I've got to go."

Her feet plopped to the floor. "What's wrong?" she asked with panic laced through her voice.

"Anxi's in trouble."

She flicked on the light. Her forehead crinkled. "What are you talking about? Did you have a bad dream?"

"Yes… I mean… Listen. I can sense things, remember?" He pulled on his boots. "Someone's taking Anxi. I have to help her."

Her brows shot up in fright. "You can't go out there."

Terk grabbed his bow and quiver of arrows. "They're taking her *right now*. I have to get to her before they're gone." Washi's words jumped into his head, but Anxi didn't have any time to lose. "Go to the bell tower and call the constable," he called out to Baba Airi as he ran outside.

Gaichu joined him.

Terk halted. "No! Get back in there." The pup cocked his ears. "Chusho." Terk picked him up, tossed him inside, and slammed the door.

Gaichu's muted barking lessened as Terk sprinted into the night. The stars provided little light, but the flat ground allowed him to run at full speed.

He let his senses guide him. Around the barn and through the field, he ran. Upon reaching the forest, he paused and considered his path. Trails formed by small animals crisscrossed the entire island. Since he had no time to fight the brush, he chose an open trail that headed in her general direction instead.

Anxi's terror sharpened. The sensation heightened his determination. Despite the deep darkness under the canopy of trees, he picked up his pace. Leaves and branches slapped him, some cutting into him, but he didn't care.

His senses didn't recognize the people who had her. Their emotions radiated annoyed purpose, but thankfully no hostility or lust. That meant little, though. They were probably just the grunts. It was their customers Anxi had to beware of.

He wouldn't let them take her.

The trail sent him on a wide arc, but it didn't concern him. The darkness did. His depth perception worsened at night. Something, possibly a log, blocked his path. He leapt, misjudged its location, and tripped, landing face down on the hard, dry dirt. Rocks cut into his forearms.

None of it mattered. He scrambled to his feet and charged onward. Rapid yet deep breaths gave him enough oxygen to maintain his speed. He broke through the jungle to the beach without slowing. Not even the sandy ground hindered his haste.

He darted to the right and leapt onto a rocky outcropping. His fingers gripped the weathered stone. His toes found purchase. The climb was easy despite the darkness. Feel. Grab. Pull. Over and over.

One last heave and he hauled himself over the lip. *Damn it*. The craggy rocks gave him pause. Without light, he couldn't distinguish shadows from depressions. He slowed, making sure of his landing before jumping from spot to spot.

He misjudged again and slipped. His knee cracked against the stone. He clenched his teeth to keep from crying out. The men were close. Anxi's desperate cries carried through the air. He had to get to her.

Softer ground met his feet. He ran on with a limp. Water runoff mixed with silt and sand made it treacherous—and noisy. He slowed further, watching out for deeper waters that would make a splash.

"Get that bitch in there," someone yelled.

Terk crept through the mangroves. He breathed, deep and quiet, wishing the insects would resume their night songs. Ducking to a break in the bushes revealed a long, cylindrical vessel half submerged in a cove. Several times bigger than Baba Airi's simple dwelling, it was still smaller than an independent cargo ship, but like nothing he'd ever seen.

The opening on top emitted some light. If the slavers had arrived from underwater, a ship with a dorsal entrance made sense.

Three people wearing a mismatch of old clothes struggled with a fourth on the vessel's surface. Two of the men looked exactly as they had in his dream. Baffled, he almost lost his balance. *How in the hell is this possible?* Nothing like this had ever happened before.

Anxi screamed a string of curses as the slavers wrestled her under control and attempted to force her down the hatch.

Chusho! He was too late. Getting her away from them would be damn near impossible now.

"No!" she bellowed. Blood ran down her chin.

"Get her in there, damn it!" The third man wore a tattered red uniform-like jacket. A glint of light caught his eye and Terk's chest hitched. It was cybernetic, like the one he used to have before cutting it out.

He pulled out an arrow and aimed as the men struggled to shove Anxi in. He thought he had the cybernetic man in his sights but hesitated. The breeze coming off the ocean was strong. If he shot at them and missed, he might hit her. Revealing his position was another possibility. The bulks on their belts indicated they were probably armed with ballistic or phaser weapons. Even if he struck one, he didn't have a chance if the other two opened fire.

Damn it. He had to do something, but what?

Anxi's terrified determination dominated his senses, but other emotions trickled in too. Not just those of the three irritated men either. He focused his ability. Three more were inside. One was in what was likely the cockpit. Another was under Anxi, probably trying to pull her in. And the third was at the back. This one's mood was despondent. The familiar reek of his lifeforce identified him as Xiaobo.

No one else, though. Washi had said others were abducted, which meant this underwater ship could be meeting with another vessel somewhere.

If he couldn't stop this here and now, he might have one more option. It wasn't a good one, but the only one he had. He took aim once again, but not at the men, and hoped the sounds of their cursing would disguise his actions. With a relaxed exhale and a quick release, he sent an arrow flying into the brush on the other side of the cove. To his relief, a loud clunk resounded.

"What was that?" the more muscular of the three men said.

"Might be an animal."

Terk held his breath. This had to work.

"That's not an animal noise," the cyborg replied. His muted emotions resembled other cyborgs Terkeshi had met. That they were still evident meant he was more human than machine.

"Should we go check it out, Cap?"

Yes. Go, you dumbasses. Terk stayed low as the cyborg scanned the jungle. If his mechanized eye was anything like Terk's had been, he'd have all sorts of applications to enable him to see beyond the darkness. So long as he kept that eye roving the other way, Terk remained hidden.

Anxi yelped as they finally shoved her inside.

"Bull, get in there and get that troublesome girl in a cage," the cyborg yelled. "Barty, let's go check it out. Maybe some fool thinks to rescue her, and we can catch us a bonus."

Terk was that fool, but he wouldn't give up.

They hopped down on the other side of the vessel and out of Terk's sight. A slosh indicated they'd likely landed in a raft, followed by sounds of paddles churning through water. He puffed and hung his bow and quiver over his shoulder. A tree beside him had a thick limb that leaned over the water. He leapt onto the trunk and scrambled up, taking care that his bow didn't catch on any branches. The light coming from the vessel guided his way.

He reached a point where the branches were too thick to continue and squatted. The gangplank was too far out, but jumping over to the vessel might be possible. However, gauging the distance might be a problem.

He focused his senses. The two men were still out searching but would return any moment. He had to do this now and hope for the best. He huffed, then lunged.

His feet landed on the metal ship and slipped. His heart leapt to his throat. He clawed for purchase. Thanks to the webbing that covered it, he gripped on and clambered to the top.

He listened beyond his hammering heart for anyone who might've heard him, then scampered over to the hatch and glanced inside. The space was dully lit. He couldn't tell from this angle whether he'd have a place to hide, but he had to chance it. If he was lucky, he could lie in wait until someone neared. Then he'd disarm them and eliminate the rest one by one.

Wait. Could he operate this kind of vessel? Did watercraft have the same controls as air or spaceships? What about the others who'd been abducted? If he took over this ship before its planned rendezvous, how would he figure out where they were?

This is stupid. But he didn't have any better ideas and so stepped onto the first rung of the interior ladder.

6
Trackers

A gnat flew into Washi's eye. He stopped with a curse and rubbed it. The grit scraped his eyeball, causing it to water. *I hate this jungle.* It might be cooler at night, but the bugs were just as persistent.

His younger brother halted. "You coming?"

Washi sighed and jogged the short distance to catch up. "This is pointless. We can't be sure he went this way."

"Baba Airi said she saw him run down this trail, and it leads to the beach," Michio said.

"We haven't seen a single sign."

Michio flicked his flashlight down the path. "Those might be his footprints."

"They could be the footprints of anything."

"Are you saying we shouldn't try?" his brother asked with incredulity in his voice.

Washi grunted, signifying neither yes nor no. "I told him not to go after them."

"He can sense the emotions of others, remember? That means he has the best chance of finding the ones behind this."

"It was reckless. What will he do when he catches up to them? He's a good fighter, but not good enough to take on a bunch of thugs."

The light shone on a log over the path. Michio pointed to the other side, revealing fresh depressions. "Looks like someone fell here."

"That's what the idiot boy gets for running through the jungle in the dark."

"What would *you* have done?"

A bitterness filled Washi's mouth. He had no answer for that. Well, he did, but he didn't want to admit it.

They continued onward. A swarm of gnats followed them every step of the way. Insects that Baba Airi called cicadas trilled in a loud and eerie unison, making his teeth ache.

"This may be a good thing," Michio added. "We've had no luck finding these people. Terkeshi caught them in the act."

"Perhaps, but if he gets captured or killed, it's his own damn fault."

Michio's flashlight reflected off the eyes of a small furry creature, sending it dashing back into the brush. "Why are you being so hard on him? None of this is his doing."

Washi harrumphed. "He got Father killed."

Michio halted and turned to him with an uncharacteristically dark expression. "What the hell are you talking about? The emperor is to blame."

Washi's temper ignited. "Terkeshi was the one who blew up that emitter."

"You mean *that weapon?*" Michio stepped into Washi's personal space. "The one the emperor wanted to use to destroy *planets?*"

Washi wilted inwardly but didn't back down. "That's not our business. The emperor's sons or not, Terkeshi and Jori roped us into committing treason. Look where it got us." He waved his hand at the surrounding forest. "We were exiled to this shithole. Jori is dead and now so is our father."

"You selfish chima." Michio's eyes blazed. Washi pulled back in surprise. Before his indignation fully formed, Michio continued. "Planets! Billions of people murdered just so that homicidal maniac can boost his pathetic ego." He jabbed his finger and advanced, making Washi step backward. "We supported Jori's plan because it was the right thing to do. We all knew the risk, even him. Even Father."

"Was it worth it?" Washi asked. "Look at how much we've lost."

"Yes, damn it. And I bet if we could ask Jori and our father that question, they'd say the same."

Washi emitted a noncommittal grunt.

"What?" Michio pulled back. "You don't agree? Maybe *you* would've preferred to continue serving that chima, but I'd rather die than support genocide. If we lost something because of it, at least we did it with our honor intact."

Sufficiently chastised, Washi looked away. He still wouldn't admit anything, though. His life had been mangled beyond recognition, and he hated every moment.

Michio glowered at him a little longer before turning away in a huff. "Come on. Let's go."

Washi followed in sullen silence. Gnats pelted his face and buzzed in his ear. One flew up his nose, but he barely noticed.

As he examined the knot in his stomach, he realized it was worry. His world had crumbled when Jori died. It shattered when he learned of his father's death. Now that rash idiot Terkeshi was running headlong into a battle he couldn't possibly win.

The night brightened somewhat when they reached the beach and emerged from the jungle into starlight. The sand spread out before them a short distance and a glass-like sea stretched into the horizon. Michio flashed the light on the loose sand, straining to find footprints.

Washi pulled out a scanner and aimed it down the flat side of the beach. "Nothing."

"This way, then." Michio pointed to the rocky outcropping. "It makes sense they wouldn't just be out in the open."

They climbed the stone, grunting but not talking. Washi wanted to think it was because they had to keep quiet, but his brother's rebuke stung worse than the bite of a giant ant.

Michio had a different personality. Washi considered himself serious and practical. Michio was responsible, but his attitude suggested a more playful and perfunctory side. Generally, their differences complemented one another. They were as close as two brothers could be.

Recent events had created a rift between them and they drifted apart. The fun-loving nature of his younger brother grated on his nerves more often. And now Michio's normally easy manner had exploded into anger—something that almost never happened.

If Washi didn't mend their relationship, he'd suffer yet another loss.

They reached the top, staying low. A small delta fanned out before them. The dark rivulets of water were almost indistinguishable from the black silt. If not for the starry reflection, he wouldn't be able to tell the difference. There was no sign of any ships, but Washi scanned anyway. Still nothing.

Michio pointed to the cluster of trees with twisting roots above the water. "Let's keep going."

They squelched through the mud with quick yet quiet steps. Washi's heart pounded with both effort and anticipation. What would they find on the other side of those trees? Nothing? A boat full of hostiles? Terkeshi's body?

Climbing over the mangrove roots proved difficult in the dark. Washi slipped. The splash set off a series of smaller splashes as little animals scattered.

The trees parted into a clearing. His scanner still didn't pick up anything, but the shadows unnerved him. He unholstered his primitive firearm, the only weapon he was allowed to have, and hoped for the best.

Michio scanned the area with his flashlight. "Look at that." He pointed to a spot of churned mud. "Something was here."

"Chusho." Washi searched the ground for clues. He found only boot prints, dents and scrapes showing signs of a possible struggle, and places smooth enough to have been created by the hull of a vessel. At least there were no bodies. "They're gone."

A gnawing sensation writhed through his gut. They'd taken Terkeshi too. A big strong boy like that would fetch a high price in the slave markets. The thought of him working mines rekindled his anger. The emperor had done this too. Not directly, of course, but he was the one who allowed slavery to thrive. He was the one who pressed his boot on the necks of all people, including his own children whose only way out had been to rebel.

Washi remembered all those times he'd stood by and watched as the emperor berated those boys with both verbal and physical abuse. He'd worried such treatment would eventually turn them into monsters too—especially Terkeshi with his hot temper. It'd made his heart ache to see them exposed to such poison. When Jori had begged him to help save lives, it hadn't taken much to convince him—nor Terkeshi. That boy had found his humanity again. How could he be angry about that?

Washi swallowed his pride. "You're right."

Michio's brows tilted into a question.

"About Jori, Terkeshi, and our father." Washi glanced off to the side, unwilling to meet his younger brother's eyes. "They acted with honor. I've just been feeling sorry for myself."

"Enough said." Michio clapped his shoulder. "Let's focus on getting Terkeshi back."

Washi followed the scraped soil out to the water and scanned the vast ocean. *How in the hell will we do that?*

7
Stowaway

Terkeshi held his breath as he climbed down inside the watercraft. The stark difference in light hurt his eye, so he closed it and hoped his senses were right about the slavers being too busy elsewhere.

When his feet reached a flat surface, he braved a glance. The meager surroundings caused his heart to skip a beat. Where would he hide?

Chusho. This was a bad idea.

The click of a door triggered him to flinch. He dove behind some sort of freestanding metal mechanism and crunched down, barely low enough to be hidden. Footsteps echoed throughout the hull of the beast. He remained frozen, not even daring a peek.

"Damn girl," a male voice grumbled as he rummaged for something. A tearing noise might've been him opening a bandage pack. Terk hoped so. These thugs had it coming. Neither Anxi nor Xiaobo deserved this fate… Well, Anxi certainly didn't.

The clomp of boots on the metal flooring retreated. A clack followed and Terk puffed. Now to find a better hiding place.

The interior was small but open. Several electronic and mechanical contraptions attached to the hull ran along this side. They'd strapped hardware and supplies above and between them wherever possible.

A locker stood across from him. If he broke the lock, they might notice. Bunks hinged on the walls to its right. Beyond those, the space narrowed. The cockpit probably resided beyond. To the left of the locker was a mini kitchen complete with cupboards, sink, and dining area. Further along, a door led to where he sensed the two villagers.

Chusho. He'd have to make do here. With the pipes and conduits connecting the mechanisms and with the stuff packed between, he might fit into a cranny and remain unseen—unless someone looked too closely.

Would they notice if he shifted this junk around? Surely not.

He shoved his bow in a crack between their things and jumped to work, being as quiet as possible. The rope reeked of seaweed, but a little finagling of the coils would help hide him. He shouldn't unwrap the emergency blankets but rearranging them gave him extra space and added cover.

The sensation of the returning slavers aggravated his urgency. He thought fast, not wanting to be exposed, and tucked himself between the wall and a waist-high barrel. Whatever was inside, it was heavy. He pushed, but the barrel barely moved. He hunkered below its center of gravity and tried again with a grunt. It moved. The grating noise seemed loud compared to the approaching voices of the men outside.

"We wasted enough time already," a man said with authority. "Let's get the hell off this shitty clump of dirt."

Terk gritted his teeth and shoved. The scrape of wood on metal was even louder. He scrambled into the hiding spot and hoped for the best.

A boot clicked as the first pirate-slaver stepped onto the entrance ladder. Terk wiggled back as far as possible, but his feet and knees were still exposed. *Please don't let them notice me.*

"Chongan!" the captain bellowed. "Let's go!"

"Aye, Captain!" a man's voice resounded from the cockpit.

The two men moved on with no indication that they saw him. Terk allowed himself to breathe once more. *Damn. Now what?*

The ship's engines fired up. The loud humming and vibration quivered to his bones. A grinding tremble and a pulling sensation from inertia followed. His ears popped. Shortly after, the ride smoothed, making him wonder whether they were moving at all.

An ache settled in his legs as he crouched. Sweat trickled down his spine from his overtaxed heart and the stuffy air. Breathing became a controlled effort, lest he make too much noise.

The nervousness agitating his gut was nothing compared to Anxi's or Xiaobo's. The added fear exuding from Xiaobo was almost as strong as Anxi's fury. Terk imagined him cowering in the corner of a cage while she paced hers like a blackbeast. If he could get to her, she'd be a great help in fighting these chimas.

He peered between two pipes. The men named Barty and Bull rummaged through the kitchen cupboards. A third man with curly black hair and bushy beard joined them. Like them, he wore a sidearm. Adding that to the small space where any noise would alert the others, Terk's plan to eliminate the crew one at a time was too risky.

After a few grunts and paltry words, the men sat at the table with their food and drinks. At first, they spoke of mundane things, but when they mentioned the girl, Terk's ears perked.

"She ain't much to look at, but she's young enough to fetch a good price," the one with curly hair said.

"Cap says we ain't takin' 'em to slavers," Barty replied.

Terk frowned. *Who, then?*

"I know. I'm just saying it's a waste." The curly haired man made a crude gesture.

"It ain't a waste when we're getting paid more for selling to these freaks," Bull said through a mouthful of food.

A shiver ran down Terk's spine.

"Freaks?" Barty frowned as though offended but his emotions remained mild. "Cap's got a cybernetic eye. These folk ain't much different."

Bull harrumphed. "The eye is one thing. That man had ports in the back of his head. The entire lower part of his partner's body was a machine."

Terk broke out into a cold sweat. The pattering in his chest made him lightheaded. He couldn't deal with more cyborgs. Not again.

"But what I mean by freaks," Bull continued, "is what they're using these folk for."

Blackness drew into Terk's vision. His breath erupted in rapid bursts. It took little imagination to guess what the cyborgs intended. Getting sold to work in mines or brothels would be horrible, but the thought of being turned into a machine put him in a panic almost too powerful to overcome.

Get a hold of yourself. He clenched his fists and gritted his teeth. His body tingled as though being pricked by icicles. The blackness lessened.

"You hear that?" one man asked.

Terk held his breath as the trio glanced around. Oddly, the fear of discovery didn't have the same effect as being reminded of his experience with cyborgs. The terror that had almost smothered him dulled and became more manageable, allowing him to focus on remaining silent and motionless.

"Hear what?" Bull asked.

"Something like hissing." Barty shrugged. "Maybe a vent cover is loose."

They returned to their plates. The conversation turned to a different topic and Terk breathed easy.

The ride dragged on as he cramped in one spot. Every noise agitated his nerves. Even his own heart seemed loud. More than once, a wave of dizziness threatened to overtake him.

Eventually, a tug of inertia told him the ship was headed upward. The engines cut out, then a subtle shift in motion indicated the vessel had surfaced and now floated atop the water. The floor beneath Terk's feet bobbed and swayed, making his stomach queasy. This was the same as when he'd traveled to the island with those fishermen, which meant… *Chusho*. He might be on a boat now.

Activity around him bloomed. The cybernetic captain barked orders and the crew completed final safety checks. Back and forth they bustled, too busy to notice Terk's hiding spot. Before long, the men brought out their prisoners. Xiaobo and Anxi's bonds required they be half carried. Anxi growled through her gag. Her eyes practically shot flames at her captors.

Terk stayed still as the hatch opened. The stale air rushed out while the fresh air dove in. The short-lived breeze cooled his forehead, followed by another bout of perspiration as the slavers hauled their prisoners up. Terk closed his eyes and hoped no one spotted him.

They carried Anxi up much quicker than they'd stuffed her in. The others hurried out next, probably eager to get out of this can.

The cyber-captain took the rear, reigniting the quivering of Terk's nerves. Some cybernetic eyes had a wider degree of vision. Terk might be seen even if the man never looked his way. His throbbing heart threatened to burst with each step on the rungs.

The captain's head breached the opening and disappeared. Terk puffed. Before he had a chance to consider the next part of his plan, the lights switched off and the hatch closed.

The shock of being alone in pitch darkness almost sent him into a panic. He angrily shook it off. It would've been worse if they'd caught him.

He left his hiding place, wanting to burst out with the gusto of a blackbeast released from its cage but using caution instead. His muscles protested and his bones cracked. The ache sharpened, then flittered away with each step.

However, his queasiness remained. He held his gut and wished this was a spaceship rather than a boat. Dealing with heavy g-force might be harder on the body but he'd take that over this unrelenting undulation any day.

He swallowed the nausea and planted himself in the middle of the room. *Now what?* With his hands on his hips, he looked up as though searching the darkness for answers. Most likely, the hatch discouraged outsiders from getting in rather than the other way around. And since everyone had disembarked, they had to go somewhere. He suspected a boat but had to be sure. It'd also be good to know whether they were in a harbor or still out at sea. If he could do this without poking his head out, that'd be ideal.

He closed his eye more from habit than necessity and concentrated his sensing ability. Dozens of lifeforces flickered in his mind, enabling him to pinpoint their locations and gauge the emotional atmosphere.

Possibly as many as four decks of people took up a space ten times the size of this watercraft, but none beyond. Since most congregated in a few areas, remaining unseen might be possible. Xiaobo and Anxi had been placed with others at the very bottom corner of his perception. The out-of-the-way area would increase his chances of being discovered and decrease their ability to escape.

His eye fluttered open with a revelation. Once he rescued them, how would he get them back to the island? He could fly just about any craft ever invented. Airships, jets, cargo ships, spaceships, and even warships. But piloting a boat was another matter that required a different type of navigation. Two-dimensional travel was easy on foot, but an ocean had no landmarks.

He pinched his bottom lip and wished he had room to pace. Taking out the crew members one at a time was still a terrible idea. He'd probably get away with it for a while, but there were too many. They'd eventually catch on and hunt him down.

When storming a spaceship, the objective was usually to get control of the command center. Doing that with a bow and arrow would be damn near impossible. What if he found a weapons locker? Would he be able to break into it? Or could he sneak up on someone and confiscate their weapon? And what if he managed to take over the command deck? How would he defend it? Plus, he still didn't know if he could operate a watercraft. Should he rescue the villagers first and hope one of them knew how?

He groaned. The problem was too big, and strategy had never been his strong suit. What would Sensei Jeruko do?

A pang bloomed in his chest. Sensei Jeruko couldn't help him anymore. He was dead. If Terk didn't think of something soon, he would be too.

8
Belly of the Beast

The sinking feeling in Terkeshi's gut spiked with a realization. Sensei Jeruko wasn't able to help him but maybe his sons could. Since Washi was already looking for the missing people, Terk needed to find a way to contact him. First, he had to sabotage the vessel before it reached a port.

He smacked his fist into his palm. That settled it. With his objectives decided, he refocused on the crew's locations. None were near him, so he retrieved his bow and quiver of arrows and slung them over his shoulder. After groping through the dark for the ladder, he climbed up and fumbled around for the opening mechanism. Luckily, it was easier to unlatch than an airlock. With a click and a hiss, the hatch lifted.

A pinkish sky with a vast ocean reflecting the same hues greeted him. To his dismay this underwater craft hadn't just parked alongside a larger one. It had been hauled up and secured to the outside with several steel cables as thick as his wrist.

The bigger vessel's hull overwhelmed him. He had no knowledge of boat layouts, and so no idea where to find a communication station. The engine room would likely be in the lower aft section, so perhaps he should go there and commit sabotage first. But with it getting lighter out, his priority was finding a hiding spot. He scooted out of the hatch and closed it, careful not to let it slam.

He grabbed a cable and hauled himself up, hating how it held heat and irritated the scar on his palm. The climb was still easy. He reached for the pulleys and other mechanisms connecting to the top. After balancing himself and using the crook of his arm to remain stabilized, he peeked over the deck.

A long, narrow breezeway with a railing on one side and a superstructure on the other led to the bow and stern. The structure had no doors that he saw. He could follow it in either direction, but the opposing decks appeared so open from this vantage that he might be exposed.

Someone appeared in his line of sight. He ducked with a curse. Aft was no longer an option. He verified the person was gone and hopped onto the deck. He hugged the wall and slunk along toward the bow. An emergency kit similar to those found on spaceships was attached to the superstructure's side. So was a round thing connected to a rope that might have been a water rescue device. Rather than continue onward, he used the kit and device as hand and footholds, hauling himself up to the roof to get a better view. His range of vision multiplied but left him more exposed than expected. A tower with wide windows rose above him at the bow.

Panic seized his chest. The people inside faced away, but how long would that last? Rather than go back, he scrambled to a previously unseen opening in the superstructure and glanced down. An empty stairwell descended into darkness. His senses didn't detect anyone, so he jumped and headed down.

He reached a wide room. The air was hotter here, practically suffocating him. A sourness like body odor mixed with salty oceanic air permeated the space. Cabinets, storage nooks, and secured crates provided a jumble of places to hide. He had to keep moving, though. If this boat docked some place, it'd ruin his chances of calling for help.

An hour of sneaking toward engine noises finally paid off. The stress had tightened his muscles to near snapping point, but he endured. Giving up now would be almost as idiotic as how he'd gotten himself into this mess.

His self-criticism shot up when he reached the engines. *What the hell?* These archaic things must've come out of the dark ages. He sniffed. A rotten acidic scent indicated the use of biofuel. He would've sneered with contempt if he had any idea how to sabotage something this low-tech.

With a sigh, he wandered around the many pipes, conduits, broad cylinders, and rectangular electronic boxes that all connected to a huge metal construct. The floor vibrated under his feet as he ducked or pulled back to hide from random workers. When he found an open toolbox, he grabbed a heavy wrench and a long screwdriver.

A smaller machine with wires and components exposed provided him with an accessible opportunity for sabotage. He glanced about. Nobody was around, so he tiptoed over. The first nut loosened easily. He grunted with effort at the second one, but it wouldn't budge. With no electronic tools in sight, he was forced to move on. He found a module with several wires connecting to various other places—a larger machine behind it, a plug to its left, and another part to its right. Removing it proved much easier.

He stepped back. Nothing changed. Perhaps it'd cause a cascading failure later, but later might be too late.

A passing worker flicked through Terk's peripheral vision, making him duck. He held his breath and waited. Something else caught his eye. Bolted to a nearby machine was a cylindrical device with two dials. He didn't know what they controlled, but if he changed their settings and removed the component, something was bound to go wrong.

The worker moved on. Terk stretched between the piping and adjusted the dials. They clicked as he turned them as far as they would go. Nothing happened, but maybe it would soon, so he worked on the bolts. The first two twisted off with ease, but he strained to unscrew the third. His senses alerted him to another worker approaching. He scurried back, leaving the device hanging.

The man whistled a merry tune as he entered the area Terk had just vacated. There wasn't much space. One more step and he'd discover his hiding place. Terk gripped his wrench and prayed he wouldn't notice the dangling piece either.

The man's shrill song slowed as he fiddled with something. The worker's emotions emitted no sign that anything was amiss, and he eventually walked away, still whistling.

Terk's shoulders relaxed. He eased out of hiding and resumed. A few seconds after, the bolt popped off, allowing him to disconnect the wires. It dropped into his hand, almost too heavy to hold. He turned it around, examining it. Its innards revealed a mess of electronic components, but no clues to its purpose.

A grinding noise reverberated through the engine room. An alarm sounded. Terk's chest hitched. Using his senses to determine the safest direction, he darted out. A spurt down a short hall led him to another room. Packed shelves took up the wall around a closet door. He opened it, finding just enough space to duck inside and hide behind a stack of junk. The door closed with a click just as an echoing tromp of footsteps neared.

His heartrate pulsed, quickly at first, then slowed to a throb. People yelled and cursed, none louder than the captain. Although their voices were muffled, he suspected no one knew what'd happened or why.

The crew came and went. At some point, they'd figure out a part was missing and that someone must've taken it. He had to get rid of it. That meant returning to the upper deck. *Chusho.* With everyone bustling about, his chances of getting caught increased. On the plus side, he might find the communications room along the way.

He searched the shelf and found a long piece of dirty cloth. Adrenaline sizzled through his veins as he used it to create a harness that secured the part as well as his tools. *Now for the hard task.*

He snuck out of the closet and darted to his next task. Someone entered the peripheral of his sensing ability, forcing him to double back. To avoid others, he took a disorienting path with too many turns.

The confusion and distress radiating from the crew switched to outrage. They must've discovered the sabotage and would soon look for the culprit. Terk located a stairway and bounded up.

He darted to the left, then found himself in a long corridor lined with wooden doors. Before making it halfway down, his sensing ability alerted him to men converging from either side. He tried the nearest doorknob. It was locked. The next was too. He gripped the third one and jostled it with rapid desperation. It wouldn't open.

Chusho! He had nowhere to hide. Someone would turn the corner and see him at any moment. He focused his senses and determined forward would confront him with just one person. Surely, he could handle that. He considered his bow but rejected the idea. With the way his aim had been off lately, he dared not risk it. If he didn't make a clean shot, the man might cry out and alert all his buddies. Terk needed to end this as silently as possible. Too bad he didn't have a knife. His wrench would do nicely, though.

A gangly man with a straggly beard rounded the corner. "What the—"

Terk struck him in the temple. The man grunted and stumbled. Terk snatched him and wrapped his arm around his neck. He squeezed with determined ferocity while dragging him away.

The man struggled at first, flailing his arms and kicking out his legs. He pounded the wall and thumped the floor with his foot a few times, but the noise didn't seem to alert anyone.

The pain of imminent death screamed through Terk as though he experienced it for himself. He held on despite the overwhelming and excruciating sensation.

When he was sure the man's lifeforce had gone, he loosened his hold. Nausea rolled in his gut as his own self-awareness returned. He turned it outward, surprised to find no one else in the immediate vicinity.

He searched the body, finding no weapons—not even a knife. Terk was stuck with a wrench and a useless bow. He grasped under the slaver's arms and hauled him off. Thankfully, the man had a light build, allowing Terk to get him up another set of stairs.

Relief swept over him together with the ocean breeze. He was back where he'd started.

A quick glance out the stairwell and down the breezeway revealed no one. He yanked the man onto the deck, then hauled him over the railing. A thump sounded as the body struck the watercraft hanging below. A splash soon followed. Terk unwound the machine part. With a mighty heave, he tossed it overboard. It fell through the small gap between the vessel and the boat, dinging against the metal crafts before falling into the ocean depths.

His tension drained. Those chimas wouldn't be able to leave now. *Unless they have a spare.* His muscles tightened once more. He might've killed that crew member for nothing—not that those who abducted innocent people deserved to live. Still, guilt twinged in his gut.

Fuck him. Terk shook it off. He had to hurry and find a communication station. He glanced about and tried to guess its location. There was that tower, but it was too open. Surely, they had a backup room somewhere.

He returned to the stairwell and headed back down. Time ticked by with agonizing slowness as he meandered between the crates toward the bow. The containers became smaller, forcing him to crouch. His stress heightened at the increased difficulty of staying hidden. Three men searched nearby. One came close enough for Terk to hear his breath. He darted around a box of supplies to avoid him.

"Hey!" the man yelled.

Terk's heart jumped and zapped him into flight mode. He bolted away, too terrified to curse his luck. Footsteps pounded behind him, threatening to damn him to the same fate as his friends.

9

The Other Major

Morning birds created a cacophony of shrills and screeches as though protesting the new day. The dull orange sun rose above the treetops, dispelling the cooler night air and replacing it with a sogginess that weighed Washi Jeruko down. He swatted at the gnats flying in front of his face as he trudged to the house where two unpleasant tasks awaited.

The voices inside reverberated with a mirth that wouldn't last. He entered, facing the trio at the table. The laughter halted. Jingyu and his mother kept their smiles, but the full lips of the woman in the middle curved down. Even though he'd tried to hide his regret, she was much better than Terkeshi at sensing emotions.

He bowed to her and remained downcast.

"What is it?" Terkeshi's mother asked, her dark, narrow eyes tilted in concern.

He tightened his hands to keep from fidgeting. "I have bad news."

Amarante rose and put her hand to her heart. "Is Terk alright?"

Washi glanced at his feet, then forced himself to face her. "Slavers took him."

Her legs buckled and she grasped the back of Jingyu's chair. "No." She clapped her hand over her mouth while tears welled in her eyes. "This can't be. I just got him back." The others hastened to her side. Washi's mother put her arm around her waist and patted her shoulder.

He inhaled and exhaled slowly, trying to gather his thoughts. "Baba Airi says he woke in the night with a panic, said someone was being taken, then rushed out the door. He's nowhere to be found but—"

Amarante held up her palm and closed her eyes. He shifted his feet and waited.

45

She eased upright and met his gaze with the soberness of the nobility. Although her expression calmed, the effort put into it seemed forced. "I can't sense him, but my range only goes so far. Are you sure they took him?"

Her tone hinted she feared something worse. An ache swelled in the back of Washi's throat. She must be hurting so much. Finding out one son was dead, then having the other sent miles beyond her reach must be as painful as his own grief over losing his father. And now Terkeshi was gone, and it was all Washi's fault for sending him to that farm.

He swallowed. "Not a hundred percent, but it seems likely. He sensed them and there are signs that he followed them. We found the area where we think something big came inland. We also found a spent arrow that could be Baba Airi's."

Jingyu cocked his head. "You located where they're putting in?"

"Yeah. An estuary to the west. It's deep and wide enough for a vessel to come in."

"You still believe it's a submarine?"

"It explains why the sensors picked nothing up."

Jingyu clasped his hands behind his back. "If we know where they're landing, we have an idea which direction to begin our search."

"Not if they traveled around the island to fool us."

"Yes, well…" The major rested his hand on Amarante's shoulder. "I'm sure we have people out there looking for them now."

Washi cleared his throat. "If we do, I'm not aware. I asked Major Whang to let us use the watercraft. He said no, that he'd handle it. That boat hasn't moved and no airships have either. I'm getting nervous. What if the slavers are done here? If we don't find them soon, we may never see our people again."

"I agree," Jingyu replied, but didn't provide the assistance Washi had hoped for.

He clenched his teeth and braced himself for the second unpleasant task. "I hate to ask this, but can you talk to him? Make sure this is a priority? And convince him to let me aid in the search?"

Amarante grasped Jingyu's upper arm. "Please. I can't lose another son."

Jingyu's brow furrowed. "I can, but if he says he'll handle it, he probably will."

Washi leaned in. "*Probably…* That's what worries me. We need to do this as soon as possible."

Jingyu sighed. "I agree. I really do. But…"

"But Major Whang isn't taking this as seriously as we are."

Jingyu's eye tilted apologetically. "I'll see what I can do. I can't promise anything, though. Major Whang is in charge of this."

Washi swallowed his pride. "If you will convince him, I'd greatly appreciate it."

"Of course," Jingyu replied, his mood seeming to brighten a little.

Washi cringed inwardly. The man probably hoped he'd earned his friendship. If this worked, he likely would. Washi wasn't comfortable with this new alliance with his stepfather, but it was a small price to pay for saving Terkeshi. *Damn that boy for not listening to me.*

He shook the thought away. As much as Terkeshi pissed him off sometimes, the uncharitable opinion that the boy should suffer the consequences of his own stupidity made him realize how much it'd hurt it if he didn't get him back.

10
Rat in a Trap

Sweat dripped from Terkeshi's brow. He dashed it away. His rashness had landed him in an inescapable situation. Shoveling pig shit was the dream life compared to the threat of getting captured and sold to cyborgs.

He darted this way and that, keeping low and watching for opportunities to escape. The vast cargo hold was a trap that seemed to shrink as flurries of footsteps drummed inside.

"He went in here!" one with a rough voice bellowed.

"Get 'im!" another with a higher pitch replied.

Terkeshi held back a string of curses. Eliminating these chimas one at a time had become impossible. With these men shouting an alarm, more would come. He darted behind a crate and evaluated his situation. Using his bow would be hopeless in this crowded space. His crappy aim notwithstanding, setting it would mean stopping and giving them the opportunity to rush him.

Hiding like frightened prey would only protect him for so long. His best bet was to stay on the move and keep them guessing—and hopefully find the communications room along the way. Though how he'd storm the place was another matter.

He ducked and slunk onward, using his senses to avoid his hunters. The adrenaline coursing through him pushed back his trepidation and helped him focus. Too bad it didn't stop his self-recrimination. Washi probably considered him a fool for not contacting the constable.

He shoved the thought away. What difference would it make? He'd likely never see the man again anyway.

A possible exit loomed nearby. The opening had no door and no light emanated from it. It could be a closet for all he knew, but the arrival of a fourth man forced his hand.

He scurried over. Once inside, he straightened against the wall and waited for his eye to adjust to the dark. His heart thundered as sweat trickled down his spine.

The room took shape. At first, the crisscrossed lines in the back looked like scaffolding. But as the shadows sharpened, a series of shelves revealed themselves. His stance deflated. *Damn it.* He was trapped in a storage area.

A pursuer neared. Terk hugged the wall. His hands trembled. He squeezed them into fists, unintentionally inciting a throbbing pang through the scarred one. His hand burned so much, pulling back his bowstring would be damn near impossible.

He still had the tools, but he'd have to fight left-handed. They'd work best in proximity. He'd hoped to avoid that. The shelves were littered with junk—an ill-assortment of mechanical and electrical parts, ropes and twine, cleaners, pillow-like things that might be floatation devices, and so on. None would be any more helpful than what he already had.

A faint light caught his eye. The tension in his chest diminished at finding a ladder headed down. It made no sense for a storage room to have this, but maybe it had been something else once. Seeing how disorganized this junk ship was, it wouldn't surprise him.

He tiptoed around the shelves and groped for the wooden rungs. His first one creaked under his foot. He froze like a scared rabbit and listened with his ears and sensing ability.

The emotions of his hunters didn't change. Terk huffed with relief. He grasped the next rung and eased his weight onto it. His slow steps caused time to drag. Every little sound sent his heart fluttering.

He reached the bottom without incident. The people on this deck were far enough away to allow him to keep moving unseen. The tanks and pipes dotting and meandering around the room identified it as a waste recycling center or fuel processing station. Considering the vomit-inducing stink here, probably both.

He weaved, climbed, and crawled his way around, keeping near the wall. Halfway over a knee-high pipe, a powerful sensation blasted his senses. He stumbled and grabbed his head.

Anxi was in trouble. Her terror darkened his vision. When it returned with a flash, he no longer saw through his own eye. He was Anxi, watching helplessly as she fought two men dragging her from her cage. The same men who'd captured her wore sickly grins. The details of Barty and Bull's leathered faces and rotten teeth turned his stomach almost as much as their putrid breath.

Although he saw and felt everything Anxi did, he had no control over her predicament. Fortunately, she was a fighter. Her arm broke free and her fist crashed into Barty's mouth. Bull punched her back, sending Terk reeling.

His vision dazzled, then abruptly returned to his own situation. A rough hand grabbed his neck and shoved him against the tank. Terk's head hit with a dull clunk.

"Well, well. What do we have here? A bilge rat?"

Terk choked, partly at the pressure on his throat and partly at the cybernetic eye that practically bored into him like a motorized drill. His fright sharpened, then released when another surge of adrenaline rushed through his veins. He broke the hold and pushed off, using his elbows and fists to ram the captain away.

The cyber-freak only bumbled backward by a few paces. His eyes widened, then his face twisted into a snarl as he threw his fist. Terk blocked it and grabbed his screwdriver with his other hand. He thrust it upward, hoping to enter the fleshy area under the man's ribs, but missed.

Terk didn't let up. Left jab followed a right punch in rapid succession. The cyber-freak staved him off, his face screwed in consternation. Terk landed a blow. His fist struck something harder than bone and sent an agonizing pain through his scarred hand.

The captain's mouth curled up in amusement. "Titanium jaw. You may be faster than me, but you don't got what it takes, rat."

Terk replied with a swipe of his screwdriver.

The man attempted to block him only to have the tip tear across his cheek. A roar ripped from his throat and his hand shot up. "Enough!"

Terk halted as a circle on the man's palm glowed a menacing blue. Before he could consider what it meant, lightning erupted from it and struck his chest. He flew backward. His bow cracked between his shoulders and the impact on a low-lying pipe. The electric shock spasming his muscles warred with the blunt force hurt radiating from his back.

The captain yanked him up by the front of his shirt. "A fighter like you will fetch a nice price."

Terk tried to resist but his body wouldn't cooperate. Whatever the cyber-freak had done to him, it'd made him as ineffective as a blackbeast cub.

The man wrenched off his bow and arrows and tossed them aside. Terk helplessly endured the captain's manhandling him. The arm with the cybernetic palm wrapped around his neck and squeezed. Terk fought for air.

Other crew members showed up as the captain hauled him to the lower decks. Their crude comments and jeers angered Terk as much as they frightened him. He tried to scratch and claw but the shocking weakness had permeated his body. Just when the muscle spasms lessened enough for him to control his movements, the cyber-freak dropped him in a chair and clamped his wrists and ankles to it.

The village prisoners rattled their cages, screaming and begging for release. The captain aimed his hand-weapon at one and fired. Blue sparks struck the cage and crackled over the metal bars, making the man inside yelp.

"Shut it, ye!" the captain bellowed. "Or I'll put *you* in this chair."

Except for Anxi, who still fought Barty and Bull, the room quieted. Terk glanced at the flesh and hair stuck to the pointed and serrated implements on a tray beside him and understood their fear. But like Anxi, they wouldn't cow him. He joined her in yelling and cursing.

"Let her be!" the captain bellowed at Barty and Bull. "We got other business to attend to."

Anxi squealed as they fought to get her back into her cage. Terk jerked and tugged at the cuffs attached to the steel chair. The iron manacles had shoddy welding, but they held fast.

He roared in frustration. "You chima! I'll rip your head off!" He tried to rock the chair, but it must've been bolted to the floor. All he managed to do was waste his energy.

The captain leaned in, his breath reeking of gutted fish. He clutched Terk's jaw and shoved his face to the side. "I'd say it's bad business to maim our merchandise, but you're already maimed, aren't ya. What happened here anyway?" He let go and flicked his hand at Terk's scar.

"I used to be a freak like you," he replied, an angry tremor in his tone.

The man pulled back and chuckled. "Spunky, ain't he?" he asked the crew. They responded with low mirthless rumbles. The captain turned stony. "That spunk of yours won't last if you don't tell me what you did with that part."

Terk almost lied and feigned ignorance but lying was cowardly. Besides, the tools they'd found on him would reveal the lie. He jutted his chin and kept his mouth shut instead. His gut churned at the prospect of being tortured, but giving in would only get him killed.

Annoyance flickered through the captain's emotions, but he shrugged it off. "Ya don't tell me, I torture you and you tell me anyway, or you just tell me. Your call, rat."

Terk resisted the urge to swallow the spit that had surged into his mouth and maintained a firm jaw. He was a rat—a rat in a trap. But like a rat, he'd resist to his dying breath.

A bald man wearing a non-military blue uniform entered, making Terk flinch. The flat smile and rigid posture reminded him of that asshole cyborg who'd tried to turn him into a machine some months back. Having muted emotions seemed to be a trait of most of these freaks. The captain still had most of his, but this man didn't even have a lifeforce. He was a machine inhabiting flesh.

"Ah, Channing," the captain said. "Lookie here. We snatched you another subject. A damn healthy looking one, too."

A chill sizzled down Terk's spine. Hellish memories of his cybernetic operation flooded his thoughts. He recalled how he'd once looked with his mechanical eye and cringed.

Anxi banged on her cage door. "Subject? What do you mean, subject? You chima!"

Terk's tongue felt thick as he stared at the cyborg whose eerie smile didn't change when he turned to the girl. "Why are they injured?"

Barty and Bull shuffled their feet. "She's a fighter," Barty replied, his busted lip sticking out.

Channing cocked his head. "She's in a cage."

The captain coughed and put on his own fake smile. "A misunderstanding. The girl won't be harmed again." He shot his men a stern look.

Terk's shoulders loosened, but only a tad.

"And the young man?" Channing's flat smile remained, making Terk swallow.

The captain straightened, feigning confidence despite clear nervousness. "He took something from our engine. We have no spare. If we don't find out where he hid it, it'll take a week to get to port."

Good. This gave Washi time to search.

"I can extract the information from him without hurting him. Gordon, bring me my CPE instrument."

Terk almost choked. He'd never heard of such a thing, but it sounded unpleasant.

A short, fat man that he hadn't noticed before turned and scurried out. He had a metal plate with ports fused to the back of his head.

The captain smiled at Terk's discomfort. "You know what a CPE instrument is, don't you? It's a multipurpose cerebrum penetration device."

White-hot light seemed to explode in Terk's brain. "No! You're not using that shit on me!" He jolted and twisted as much as the chair allowed while the pattering in his chest increased. The manacles gouged into his wrists, cutting skin and bruising tendons, but he hardly noticed. He wasn't sure how it worked, but something that pierced his skull couldn't be good.

Channing remained passive. "No need for concern. It will only lower your inhibitions and encourage you to tell us what we want to know."

Terk roared and fought against his chair. It didn't sound invasive but the idea of being forced into compliance brought on a new terror. Something similar had been used on him before and caused him to murder a bunch of innocent people. He'd trained in resisting drugs and mind-reading abilities, but he had no experience against a machine.

He already suspected this Channing freak didn't want him dead, so telling his secret gained him time to find a way out of this mess. And it wasn't like they could retrieve the part.

"Calm down before you hurt yourself!" the captain bellowed. "Someone get him a sedative before he damages himself."

"No! I'll tell you, damn it!" Terk snarled. His teeth ached from biting down so hard. His body throbbed as though being prodded with electrical shocks. "I'll tell you. Just don't put that shit in me."

The captain's and Channing's smiles radiated pleasure, but one turned smug while the other merely curled up.

"Well, where is it?" The captain crossed his arms.

Terk panted, still unsure whether he should say. "I threw it overboard."

"Bullshit. We found you on the second deck. If you had time to get to the main deck, why head back down?"

"Where else would I go?" Terk replied in a frantic tone. "Into the ocean? I don't know where the hell we are. You think I'm stupid enough to get stuck in the middle of the sea with no provisions?"

"You're stupid enough to come on board, aren't ya? How'd you get here anyway?"

It was Terk's turn to be smug. "I snuck aboard your watercraft when you idiots were out searching for the arrow I shot."

The captain darkened. "Impossible!" he replied, spittle spraying from his mouth.

"He's telling the truth," Channing said.

"Well, crap." The captain spat. "Maybe we should get that CPE to make sure."

Terk's panic reignited. "I don't lie!" he yelled with a squeal. "I tossed it. It's gone."

"I don't believe you." The captain leaned in with a sneer.

"I do." Channing cocked his head. "Curious that the threat of the CPE frightens you more than torture."

"Someone tried to turn me into a freak like you before. I'd rather die than let it happen again."

"The transition is inevitable," Channing said.

The captain laughed and smacked Terk's shoulder. "Damn right it is. The only way you're getting off this boat is when we get to the port where more of these guys are waiting."

"No!" Terk yanked his hands back, again and again, hoping something—wrists or chair, it didn't matter—would break. "I won't let you do this to me! I'll kill myself first!"

"Quit your cryin', boy." The captain smacked him upside the head. "At least you'll serve a higher purpose than living on some pathetic farm in the middle of nowhere."

Channing made a sharp nod. "We're giving you the opportunity to be better, to do greater things."

"Greater, my ass!" Tears streamed down Terk's face as his tone oscillated between anger and fear. "My mind will be dead and my body will be a slave. I won't serve you freaks! I won't!"

Channing and the captain shrugged and turned away, leaving him to writhe against his empty promises. He had more to say but broke into a sob instead. A pained thought snuck by, deepening his shame. What would Washi think of him now?

11
Casual Passing

The sun beamed down like an angry god. The cloudless sky held an oppressive beauty with its solid blueness. Washi hurried despite his uniform's lack of a coolant feature. He hated how it felt when he sweated in it—and how it smelled.

He reached a shaded area beneath the spreading branches of a kapok tree. Jingyu approached from another direction. To an observer, they should appear to meet in casual passing. This encounter had been planned through a secret message to Washi's mother.

Washi wiped his palms on his thighs and tried to keep his nervous curiosity from showing as Jingyu neared. "Major," he greeted.

"Major Whang said he's not sending anyone out," Jingyu blurted.

Washi stiffened. "What? Why?" he replied louder than intended.

Jingyu gestured downward with his hand even though no one was near enough to hear them.

Washi hid his fury and dismay, smiling in a way he hoped appeared friendly to any observers.

"The rising tensions with the emperor has his full—"

"But our people." Washi's voice ejected in a rough whisper. "We finally know where to start looking and—"

Jingyu put up his hand. "I know. Which is why…" He inhaled, expanding his chest, then exhaled as though trying to gather his thoughts. "… Why I'm giving you the means to procure an airship."

Washi's eyes widened. "You mean steal one?"

"Borrow," Jingyu interjected. "With my blessing. I'll tell Major Whang I authorized this."

"But you don't have a say."

Jingyu shrugged. "No, but I have *sway*."

"So you'll accept the blame?" Washi said with incredulity.

"Don't worry. I have a good relationship with the colonel. I doubt I'll be in much trouble."

Washi opened his mouth, but he emitted no sound. He wanted to thank him, but one question kept running through his mind. "Why?"

Jingyu pulled back. "You mean, why am I doing this?"

"Yeah. Is it because Terkeshi is the heir to the empire?"

Jingyu laughed without humor. "I admit I've imagined what it would be like to have an emperor who truly cared. But I think we both know getting him on the throne will be damn near impossible. Still, the boy has potential. Not just with his skills, either. He's risked his life to save people."

"Not my father," Washi mumbled as a bitterness rose to his throat.

Jingyu tilted his head in sympathy. "I'm sure he didn't mean for it to turn out like that. The way I see it, both he and your father knew the danger of destroying the emitter and did it anyway, saving millions, possibly billions of people."

A knot formed in Washi's gut. He hated that his father was dead. He also hated how Jingyu was right. "Surely you're not taking this risk just because of Terkeshi's potential."

"No. I have other reasons."

When he didn't elaborate, Washi waved his hand in a circular motion. "Such as…"

"Your mother, for one. The boy's mother is her friend. What sort of man would I be if I let either of them down? Besides. It's the right thing to do. I get we have our hands full preparing against the emperor's threats, but allowing you to use one airship won't inhibit that. And I have a feeling Major Whang is just being spiteful."

Washi grunted in agreement. "He doesn't like me." He and the major had grated on one another's nerves right from the get-go. Washi's negative attitude about his predicament hadn't helped.

Jingyu clapped him on the shoulder. "Don't take it personally. Whang doesn't like anyone."

Washi stared off into the distance, considering the consequences. "Alright. What's to keep Whang from sending airships after me?"

"We'll coordinate so that I'm in the control tower at the same time."

"Are you sure they will break procedure?"

"They'll be a little uncomfortable, but they won't counter me."

Washi shook his head, still uncertain. "What then? If I find them, I can't rescue them by myself."

"No, probably not. Take a squad with you. And if you locate them, call it in. I'll inform the colonel so Major Whang won't risk looking like an ass by refusing to do anything."

Washi exhaled. It was a flimsy plan, but a better one than he had before. "Thank you. I can't tell you how much I appreciate this." Accepting Jingyu's offer didn't taste as bitter as he'd expected.

Jingyu produced a solemn grin. "We'll get him and the others back—no matter what it takes."

Washi bowed at an angle deeper than their differences in rank required. His resentment disappeared in a swirl of gratitude, admiration, and respect. At the same time, the angst of trying to figure out how to rescue Terkeshi was replaced with a worry that he wouldn't find him. Even knowing which direction to begin his search might not be enough. The ocean was vast, and the enemy had a head start.

"When can I leave?"

"As soon as you and your brother get a squad together."

Washi's gut did a somersault. He gathered his resolve. "Let's do this."

12
Caged

Grey swirls moved like sludge. A black maw opened at its center. Terkeshi drifted in and out of it without emotion. The darkness represented neither fear nor comfort. Memories didn't plague him. Dreams didn't haunt him. Reality was far away.

The surrounding haze was different. At first, it offered solace, like a soft blanket. Then faint blotches of light appeared. An ache bloomed. Not a terrible one. Just irritating. Dreams flashed in and out—or maybe they were memories. The lights brightened. Muffled crying grew louder. The more he became aware of it, the more despondent he felt. It wasn't his emotion, though.

Curiosity roused him. His eyelid drifted open. As his vision sharpened, the sight of several people in cages jolted him upright. His head swam and he cradled it in his palm. As the dizziness wore off, his memories returned.

He'd been fighting to get out of the chair when the cyber-captain loomed toward him, yelling. Terk had been too far into his hysteria to understand his words. Then someone else approached. Terk couldn't discern the item in his hand, but the current tightness in his brain, the dryness of his mouth, and the lingering grogginess indicated they had sedated him.

His panic still resided in his gut, ready to bound to the fore once more. He sat in a blackbeast cage. Iron bars, a crusted floor, and a caustic odor of cleaner mixed with enough shit and piss to make anyone gag. Genetically modified from Torlesian wolves, blackbeasts were huge, easily weighing over two hundred fifty kilograms. This meant he had the space to stretch out, but no room to stand.

He studied the cage for any weaknesses. But like the manacles, there were none. He was a prisoner. And if Washi didn't find him, he'd become a machine.

Despair smothered him. He never should've tried to rescue Anxi. He should've alerted the constable like Washi had told him. What a fool he was. An incompetent fool.

A sharp whisper pierced through his thoughts. "Terk!"

Anxi occupied the cage next to him. Her brow wrinkled with worry. Dried blood crusted in her nostrils, a purple-blue bruise bloomed under her eye, and her lips were cut and swollen.

"Are you alright?" he asked her.

She nodded. Her emotions carried anger, but he suspected her outrage would be greater if she'd experienced a certain type of abuse. He breathed easy, thankful his capture had interrupted those men before they used her.

"What are we going to do?" Her tone conveyed the same desperate hopelessness he held.

"I'm not sure," he replied. He pulled up his knees, leaned his head against the bars, and sighed.

"I've been trying to pick this lock, but I'm not having any luck." Anxi jerked at the padlock on her cage with frustration.

Terk blinked at the finger-length splinter in her hand. "Where'd you get that?"

She thumbed behind her where a large wooden crate sat.

"You need two of those," he said.

Her brows twisted. "If one doesn't work, how will two make it better?"

"One to align the tumblers, the other to put pressure on them so they stay in place."

"Really?"

"Yeah." The memory of the man Sensei Jeruko had hired to teach him and Jori caused his stomach to knot. Both his mentor and his brother were dead now—all because of his foolishness. He deserved to be in this cage.

"If I get another, can you do it?" Anxi asked.

Terk considered the splinter. Defeat loomed over him like a sinister shadow. They stood little chance against their captors—their fate sealed at the moment of capture.

"Please?" Anxi's eyebrows curled in. "I don't want to be a slave—or a machine."

Her fear permeated his senses. He soaked in the sharp anger that accompanied it. Giving in to the inevitable wouldn't only affect himself. There were others here. Mister Yin, a farmer who'd traded Baba Airi his chicks for one of her piglets. Nuying, the herbalist who made Baba Airi her medicine. Xiaobo, Anxi, and several more he didn't recognize. They'd all be turned into machines if he didn't do something. Plus, what would become of Baba Airi if she lost his help? What would happen to her livestock? And who would take care of that damn pup?

"Alright." Terk took the splinter. "Get me another. It needs to be thin yet strong."

She darted to the back of her cage. Her grunts combined with scratching as she stretched and dug at a jagged hole at the bottom corner of a crate. Pieces broke off. Some were too short, others too fat, and most too weak.

A sensation intruded on Terk's senses. "Someone's coming."

She swept away the evidence of her vandalism, then huddled in the back with her knees pulled close.

A squealing neared. The door clanked open, revealing a man with a cart. Piled under and on top were stacks of tins. An odor of sour bread accompanied a warm, weedy scent that resembled Baba Airi's vegetable stew. A few people stirred in their cages, but most remained despondent and still.

"Well, well, well. Look who's awake." This man was taller and leaner than the one who'd taken Anxi. He had a long, sharp nose similar to the seafaring birds who plucked fish from the shallow shore.

When Terk glowered in reply, the man put on a gloating grin that displayed the gaps between his rotting teeth. "All that trouble to slow down our ship…" He tsked. "Didn't do any good. Our cyber friends will get us going again."

The panic lurking in Terk's stomach regurgitated.

The man cackled. "I don't know what idiotic notions went through your head when you decided to stow away here, but you failed. Never met someone so stupid in my life."

Terk's cheeks burned. A flurry of embarrassment, outrage, and fear threatened to drown him.

By the time the man served everyone their gruel and left, a budding determination had pushed Terk's self-pity aside. Getting out of this mess was more urgent than ever.

Anxi resumed picking and clawing until she pulled off another finger-length splinter that seemed strong enough to work. Terk inspected the padlock on his cage. Fortunately, its keyhole accommodated both sticks. As he'd suspected, it was a tumbler lock. Its straightforward design was common among the poorer population.

He remembered complaining about having to learn how to do this. "This is stupid," he'd said to Master Teagan. "If anyone has the skill to get past my father's defenses to kidnap me, they won't use something so primitive."

"You're not considering all the possibilities," the obese man replied, his jowly chin wobbling with each word. "Knowing your propensity for not listening…" Terk bristled at the insult, but there wasn't much he could do about it. Complaining to Father wouldn't elicit any empathy. Even at the age of ten, he was expected to solve his own problems. "… What if you wander off like you did in Paxon, and some thug kidnaps you because you made it so convenient? Those kinds of people won't have state-of-the-art equipment."

Terk had replied something like that happening was ridiculously improbable. No one would be stupid enough to kidnap the emperor's son. Since he'd been third in line at the time, everyone had known Father wouldn't pay his ransom.

He'd resented Teagan's critical teachings back then, but today he was grateful. He'd never quite mastered breaking electronic locks the way his brother had, but this primitive thing would be as simple to break open as an egg.

After getting a feel for the lock's internal mechanisms, he pushed the tumblers in place. The lock opened with a click.

Anxi's eyes popped. "You did it!"

Terk's anxiety dropped a notch. Step one, complete. *Now what?*

The room erupted with restlessness the prisoners shifted from their defeated positions and pressed hopeful faces to the bars. The twenty or so people seemed like a lot until he regarded their bony frames and farm-calloused hands. These weren't soldiers. The only thing these farmers had ever fought was their own fatigue. If he let them out, they'd be more of a hindrance than a help.

They'd make a great distraction while he snuck to a communications room, but the thought of sacrificing them to save himself churned his stomach. He came here to get them out, not get them killed.

He should do this alone. But what if he had another episode where he saw through someone else's eyes? What if the slavers cornered him again and his handicaps rendered him ineffective?

He studied the prisoners once more, hoping to find somebody smart and strong enough to help him if he got into trouble. His eye fell on Anxi. Her marksmanship was—something he'd embarrassingly learned after boasting and making derogatory remarks about her being a girl. She wasn't trained in martial arts, but she had the heart of a warrior. She'd already proved her mettle when Lixin had attacked her. He had no doubt she'd fight with the same fire again.

With his decision made, he exited his cage and worked on her lock. Once she was out, he met the hopeful faces still peering at him. A pang of guilt wriggled inside him, but sense overruled it.

He sucked in air. "Listen. There are about three dozen slavers on this ship, and they're all armed. We're on a watercraft in the middle of the ocean. Escaping this cage doesn't mean escaping our situation. If anything, it puts us all in more danger."

"What about you?" someone asked.

"Where are you going?"

"So are you just leaving us here?"

Those and more questions arose, each more desperate than the last. Terk put up his hand. "I have a plan, but it won't work if we're all wandering around." He motioned to Anxi. "The two of us can sneak about much easier."

"And do what?"

Terk didn't want to answer that. If the crew discovered he was missing, they'd ask these people. No way would they hold up to torture.

"Why her?" Xiaobo said with a sneer. "She's just a girl."

Terk curled his lip with scorn. "A girl who's smarter than you and can beat you in a fight."

Xiaobo clamped his mouth shut and sulked.

"Son," an older man said. "You two are only kids. Let an adult do this."

Terk clenched his fists. He hated it when people told him that. As if being an adult somehow meant they were better at everything.

Well, he might be young, but he had a hell of a lot more experience with fighting. "Alright," he replied, pretending to relent. "What will you do if you get out of here?"

The man opened and closed his mouth.

"Take over the ship," a woman said, "and go home."

"Can you operate a boat like this?" Terk asked. "Do you know which direction to go?"

The woman looked away.

"Do you?" the same older man replied.

"I probably know more about operating a vessel than any of you." He'd spoken the truth, omitting the fact that he'd never learned to pilot a watercraft.

"Alright. Fine," the man said. "But let me go with you instead of her."

Terk shook his head. "You've all seen her fighting off these brutes. She's strong and she doesn't give up. I don't know any of you, but I know her. She's a fighter."

"You can't leave us here!" A younger man whined.

Terk growled. "I'm not. I'm keeping you safe until I figure this out."

"But if something happens to you, we're all still stuck here."

Terk huffed. "Let me be honest." He waved his hand at their surroundings. "We're already fucked. Letting you all out won't change that."

The woman jerked the bars of her cage door. "I want out!"

"Don't leave us here!" someone else yelled.

Their pleas and cries intensified. Terk clenched his jaw and pulled Anxi's arm. "Let's get out of here before their ruckus gets us caught."

She agreed with a quick nod. He pushed down on the metal doorhandle. It resisted. Most ships had locks to keep people out of a room, not in, but this one was owned by slavers. He put his weight on it. The door clicked. Terk had only a moment of relief before the prisoners' clamoring erupted. He and Anxi hurried out. When he shut the door, their cries muted. *Good.* Maybe no one would come investigate. They might have a chance.

He urged her down the corridor, using his senses to avoid trouble. They passed a few doors and were almost to a stairwell when she stopped. "This way."

"It's just a storage room," he replied.

She pointed inside. "We need weapons."

Oh. Yeah. Hands and feet wouldn't do much against armed thugs. He probably had superior combat skills, but his chances of success would increase if he found a phaser or firearm.

They rummaged through the messy room. Anxi spotted a stray pipe about the length of her forearm. Terk grabbed a rusty crowbar. They were only good for sneak attacks but better than nothing.

"Hey, look!" Anxi said in a loud whisper as she picked up a bow and quiver of arrows.

"My bow," he replied with the same hushed intensity.

"Oh yeah." Anxi pulled out an arrow. "Baba Airi made these."

Terk inspected the, surprised to find it in good shape. When he'd heard it crack earlier, he'd assumed it had broken. Continued stress might weaken it over time, but it'd work well enough for now.

He slung the weapon and ammunition over his shoulders and headed out. She followed his lead, her knuckles white and her eyes darting about.

"Don't worry," he said. "I'll sense it if someone gets close."

"Sense it how?"

Terk snapped his mouth shut. Only a few people were aware of his sensing ability. His mother was the only person these farmers knew who read emotions and he couldn't risk exposing his identity by admitting he had the same skill. "Just trust me."

"Alright," she replied in a shaky voice. "So what's your plan? Can you really operate this boat?"

"I might be able to figure it out, but finding a communications room is our best bet. There must be people looking for us already. All we have to do is tell them where we are."

"And where are we?"

Terk grit his teeth in frustration. Explaining how these things worked to a farmer was about as easy as teaching his dog to make the bed. "A radio emits a signal that can be pinpointed. Just calling for help will be enough."

"Oh. Alright. Good plan. Wait…" She halted. "Do you know how to use a radio?"

Terk sighed. "Yes, now be quiet."

The seriousness of the situation seemed to hamper her inclination to banter. Her doubts decreased while her confidence increased, but her nervousness remained. Terk's did as well. Although he'd snuck through parts of this ship already, so much could still go wrong. The other prisoners might raise an alarm. Another crew member could visit that area and see them missing. And if too many people occupied the communications room, he and Anxi wouldn't stand a chance.

He shoved his worries aside. *Mushin*. No mind. He had to remain focused. *Fudoshin*. Immoveable mind. Don't let doubt creep in.

13
Trapped

The squeak of the wooden steps twinged Terkeshi's insides. The stairway was wider and more brightly lit than the other he'd used, and he was sure someone would discover them at any moment.

The next deck up was so close, but he dared not hurry. Getting caught now would ruin what little chance they had. He pointed at the noisy step, then waved his hand. Anxi nodded, taking a long stride to avoid it.

As they hugged the stairwell's wall, movement ahead grabbed his attention. He strained to listen. Off to the left was an operations room of some kind. Although he didn't sense anything, the tops of two heads bobbed in his line of sight. *Damn cyborgs.*

Sneaking by them unseen would be difficult. Two hallways, one forward and the other to the right, provided two options—three if they headed back down to avoid the risk of being caught by cyborgs.

The sensations of people nearing from below decided it for him. He risked a glance upward. The cyborgs faced away from him. He motioned Anxi up. When she reached his side, they kept low and crawled closer to the top.

Terk pointed to the hall ahead, then put up his palm to tell her to hold on for a moment. He took another peep. An androgynous cyborg studied their screen. He ducked with a silent curse.

Clicks and taps filled the silence. Clothes rustled. When it quieted, he took another quick glimpse. Both cyborgs faced away. He waved his hand at Anxi, motioning her up. She tiptoed up at a hurried pace. The top step creaked. She bounded into the hall on the balls of her toes. One cyborg turned around. Terk cursed silently and hunkered down.

Anxi hugged the wall, her body stiff with fright. Terk held his breath. The pulsing of his blood throbbed against his eardrums. If the cyborgs suspected anything, he wouldn't know until it was too late.

The sound of work resumed. He slowly emptied his lungs and waited. If he was right, the taps meant the androgynous cyborg was working on the console and quietness indicated their attention was elsewhere.

The sounds shifted, followed by silence. He looked out. Sure enough, both faced away. He crept to the top of the stairs, careful to avoid the board Anxi had triggered. With one eye, he had a difficult time keeping a watch on both the cyborgs and the direction he needed to go. He flicked his gaze back and forth between Anxi and the enemy and prayed.

The androgynous cyborg turned their shoulder. Terk's heart leapt to his throat as he darted into the hall. If he'd made any noise, he couldn't hear it over the thumping in his chest. He stiffened beside Anxi, expecting discovery at any moment.

He didn't know how long he stood there before Anxi nudged him. She inclined her head down the hall, urging him on with an anxiousness that matched his own.

Terk shook the tingling from his fingers. He motioned with his head, and they headed down the long hallway lined with old wooden doors. The paint flaked off and the hinges were askew. One had a worn poster of a naked woman nailed to it. This and the fetid odor of unwashed bodies told him he must be in the crew's quarters. Fortunately, not a single lifeforce invaded his senses.

They reached the next deck without trouble. This one promised to be as navigable as the last, but for a different reason. He'd come full circle, back to the room with all the crates and supplies. Lots of hiding places, but damn it, he hadn't seen any hint of a communications room.

With a silent curse, he gave in and headed to the top deck. They inched around, climbed over, and crawled between boxes until they reached the stairway he had first entered.

He hesitated in the doorway. Once they stepped out, they'd be exposed. Although the ocean would greet them in the front and the superstructure would block their backs, all it would take was one person to look down the breezeway.

They stayed hidden below while Terk used his senses to locate the crew. A few dawdled in the direction they needed to go, so he waited.

Anxi elbowed him and tilted her brows in a question. He pointed as though she could see on the other side of the walls. "There're people over that way," he whispered. "I'm waiting for them to move on."

"I don't hear anything," she murmured back.

"Trust me." He spoke a little louder but not by much. "Just wait a few more minutes."

She agreed, though her emotions still carried confusion. "So…" she said. Terk braced himself, expecting her to ask for an explanation. "Did you mean what you said about me being a good fighter?"

Terk cocked his head at the unanticipated question, then shrugged. "I didn't say good, but you can best Lixin. That's something."

"If we get out of this, will you teach me more?"

Terk couldn't speak. He'd never taught anyone before and wasn't even sure where to begin. And to train a girl… It would be weird. But then again, why not? Girls had more reasons to learn to defend themselves than men. And no one else was likely to teach her. Still… "Let's get out of this mess first."

Two of the three people he'd sensed had moved on. With all the activity on this ship, this was probably his best chance. He motioned Anxi to follow, then crept from his hiding spot. Not a soul was seen or heard as they made their way out and down the breezeway, backs to the wall. After ducking below portholes, dodging stuff on the ground and darting around items hung on the wall, they reached the edge of the superstructure and stopped.

He peeked out. A man grunted while hauling a rope as thick as his forearm. Terk retrieved an arrow and notched it to his bow. His palm ached, but it wasn't that bad yet. He peered around the corner once more and aimed.

The practice he'd had the night before bloomed into his mind. If he missed this shot, the man would cry out and alert everyone. He couldn't afford to miss.

"Chusho!" he loosened his grip and pulled back behind the wall.

"What is it?" Anxi asked.

Terk bit the inside of his cheek. "My aim sucks." He handed her the bow. "You should do it."

An unsure sensation crawled through her emotions, but she took it from him. She tested the pull. "It's stronger than I'm used to."

Terk wiped his hand down his face, the sweat slicking his palm. "If I pull it back, can you hold it long enough to aim and fire?"

"Yes."

Terk helped her. He didn't need to tell her to target the heart although it was somewhat protected by the ribcage. She was a damn good hunter, and this bow was designed for hunting boars. Even if she missed the heart, which he doubted, the arrowhead would likely penetrate through bone and into a lung.

She released the arrow with a twang. The man arched backward. An abrupt muted cry escaped him. He dropped to his knees, then fell onto his face. Terk rushed in with his crowbar in hand. A swift blow to the back of the head ensured the man's demise. Although the pain of his death stabbed through Terk's senses, the adrenaline coursing through him allowed him to ignore it.

Anxi trailed behind him and together they hunched between stacks of barrels secured to the deck. The windowed tower he assumed held the control room and probably a communications device loomed in his line of sight. Since no one inside seemed to look his way, he pulled the body toward him and maneuvered it aside, retrieving the bloodied arrow.

"Now what?" Anxi asked, her eyes darting to the man she'd just killed. She didn't seem bothered by it, but Terk had no doubt it would come later. The first was always the hardest.

He pointed to the tower. "We need to get up there."

Her jaw dropped. "There's at least four people inside."

Terk's senses agreed. "Yeah."

"You want me to shoot?" Uncertainty laced through her emotions. "I don't know how thick that glass is, and the impact will alter my aim. They'll figure out where we are before we have a chance to do anything."

Terk deflated. She was right. If those men were armed—and they probably were—their chances diminished even more.

"How do we get up there?" she asked.

Terk swallowed the dryness from his throat. "I don't know." He inspected their surroundings, hoping an idea would come. None did.

An emotional alarm rose in Terk's senses. It originated from somewhere below him and spread. Shortly after, the people in the tower became more active.

He pulled Anxi down closer to the sea-salted deck. "I think they just realized we've escaped."

"What? How do you know?"

He pointed to the tower. "The men up there are restless."

She moved as though to look and he held her back. "Wait."

The emotions spread until everyone was on high alert. Thankfully, their search was mostly confined to the lower decks. Perhaps they didn't believe he'd gotten this far.

His senses followed two men as they came down from the tower and closer to his location. They didn't seem to be headed toward him, though. He caught a snatch of their urgent chatter, but their words were indistinct. He and Anxi snuck around the barrels, keeping out of view.

When the men disappeared below deck, Terk poked his head out. The two-remaining people in the tower peered out, but neither looked his way. He motioned for Anxi to follow, and they scrambled to the cover of what he assumed was a huge exhaust pipe. One man swiveled in his direction, but Terk doubted he saw him. He waited a few moments before peeking out again. They all gazed outward rather than down. Terk and Anxi dashed to the door at the bottom of the tower.

He tried the handle, relieved to find it unlocked. He eased it open, and they slipped inside. A quick glance told him no one was around. He fiddled with the doorknob but couldn't figure out how to lock it.

He huffed and turned back to take stock of the room. The edges of the entry were littered with ill-assorted junk but nothing better than the tools they'd already found. *Wait.* He picked up a palm-sized wedge and flipped it in his hand. He cocked a smile at Anxi. She responded with furrowed brows. He jammed it under the door. She dipped her head in understanding.

Before them was a spiraling staircase that would allow them to go up unseen. It was made of alloy, so no creaking wood but perhaps the groans and squeaks of strained metal. They tiptoed upward until voices reached their ears.

"I bet the idiots jumped overboard," one man said.

"Maybe," the other replied. "That boy got all the way from the sub to the engine room without us seeing him, though. They could be anywhere by now."

"Yeah, but to what end? Where would they even go?"

"Who the hell knows what goes through these dumb peasants' heads."

Terk motioned for the bow. She drew it from around her shoulder and traded him for his crowbar. He notched an arrow and pulled the string taut, hating how the tension aggravated the scar in his hand. He should let Anxi be the one to fire, but he was sure he'd be able to hit a target at such a close distance. With a quick dip of his head, he told her to get ready. Though nervousness ran through her, she gripped the tools with determination etched on her forehead.

He rushed up and fired at the closest man. He aimed for the throat but the arrow penetrated the man's cheek. The result was the same. He tumbled backward, making only a strangled sound.

At the same moment, Anxi attacked the other man. He'd been facing the opposite direction and turned only partway when the claw of her crowbar smashed into his head. He fell like a sack of rocks. She pummeled him, grunting with each bloody strike, until he stopped moving.

The pain of death flared through Terk's senses like a double-edged sword. The excruciating sensation blinded him, and he clenched his gut as though someone had tied it into a giant knot and yanked it tighter.

It passed quickly, but his stomach still churned in a typhoon. He dropped to his knees with a thud and puked. Anxi did the same. Killing a man from a distance was one thing. The brutality of this kill was worse, and her horror compounded his own.

He regained his composure, relief washing over him like a cool stream. They'd done it. They reached a place with communications equipment.

His abatement didn't last. Although he recognized which machine was the radio, it was so outdated that he had no clue how to operate it.

"Well, chusho."

14
Search Pattern

The airship rumbled as it flew into the horizon. The rays of the white sun dazzled off the crystalline sea, making it difficult for Washi Jeruko to find any ships. That and the ocean was just too vast—almost like the infinite vacuum of space but without the variously shaped and colored galaxies to break the monotony.

He ground his teeth. "If they're still on a submarine," he said to Michio in the copilot seat, "this whole thing is a waste of time."

"I doubt they'd still be on a sub. Based on what we found, it's too small to hold all the people they've abducted. They must be meeting with something bigger out beyond our radar range."

"Yeah, but who's to say it's a boat and not an airship or another submarine?"

"You're being pessimistic. Most likely, it won't be either."

"Why not? They're perfectly legitimate options."

"But unlikely. Think about it. The slaving business is complex. At its simplest, the ones kidnapping are not the same ones selling or enslaving. Chances are, this gang will take our people to one of the many slave markets on the mainland, maybe even to a middleman who will transport them further in."

"That doesn't mean they can't have a sub or airship."

"We're talking about thugs, remember? Boats are much cheaper and easier to operate."

Washi sighed. He wasn't sure whether this made sense because he wanted it to or because it actually did. They'd learned more about the slave trade than they ever had serving the emperor, but still didn't know everything.

He allowed Michio to keep his optimism while his own mood continued to sink. Flying low, he conducted a parallel track search that began a little further out than their estimate of how far the slavers could've traveled in a rudimentary water vessel, then flew back and forth an over a decreasing range that would eventually bring them back to the island.

While he kept his eyes ahead or on the controls, his brother scoured the ocean with an intense hopefulness that Washi could never hope to match. Even the squad in the cabin behind him seemed hopeful. Their laughter and energetic chatter signified their eagerness for a ship incursion and battle. A weight for not sharing the same feeling settled in his abdomen. This search was fruitless. They should just face it. Terkeshi was lost.

"Stupid boy," he mumbled.

"Don't be so hard on him," Michio replied as he peered through the binoculars. "You would've gone after them on your own too."

"I would've called and waited for help."

"You have the means. That vehicle of yours would've gotten you to the constable much faster. All Terkeshi had was his legs and that one moment."

"It was still foolish. What the hell did he think he'd achieve by himself?"

"It was his only option. And let's not forget that if he hadn't done it, we wouldn't know where to start looking."

Washi grunted. "For all the good it's doing."

"You're still angry with him."

"No, I'm not," Washi replied defensively.

"You are. I can see it every time you either talk to him or speak about him. What happened with our father wasn't his fault."

Washi gritted his teeth. He hated this argument, partly because Michio was right and partly because he couldn't let his anger go.

"You remember what it was like when we were young?" Michio asked, seemingly changing the subject. "Rash, hot-headed, thought we knew everything."

"We weren't as bad as he is."

"No, but you need to account for his upbringing. We had a father who guided us with words rather than fists. Who encouraged us, instead of constantly putting us down."

Washi's stomach somersaulted as he remembered all the times the emperor had mistreated his sons, and how he had wanted to step in and tell that chima off.

"We're his family," Michio continued. "He needs us—now more than ever."

Those words doused Washi's anger. His brother was right. If they found Terkeshi, he'd make amends. Jingyu was right too. The boy had potential. That he'd risked himself to go after the slavers didn't just highlight his foolishness, it also emphasized his desire to help others.

The radio beeped, interrupting his musings.

"Control tower to *Cormorant*. Do you read?"

"*Cormorant* here," Michio answered without taking his eyes off the sea.

"Return to base immediately, *Cormorant*."

A hardness detonated in Washi's gut, and he shot his brother a worried look.

"Negative." Michio's forehead furrowed in uncharacteristic displeasure. "We're still searching for our people."

"Sorry, Sir," the tower operator replied. "I have direct orders from Major Whang."

Washi pounded a fist on the edge of the control panel. "That chima!"

Michio lowered the binoculars and turned to Washi. "We can't give up."

"What choice do we have?" Disobeying might land him in serious trouble. But even with the ocean's endless horizon, he didn't want to stop looking. He glanced at the controls, but couldn't bring himself to change course. What was a reprimand compared to losing Terkeshi?

Realization struck him. How he felt at this moment had probably been the same for Terkeshi when he'd sensed the kidnapping. It was foolish to go on, but doing anything else was out of the question.

15
Lack of Communication

Terkeshi leaned on the console and studied the communications station. The microphone transmitter was obvious. The receiver comprised an open speaker, but the numbers and symbols on the panel weren't familiar. What did DSC stand for? Was this the option that allowed him to transmit via a specific frequency? If so, which one should he use? Where was the emergency broadcast button? He frantically tried to make sense of it all.

"I thought you knew how to use this." Anxi's hot breath irritated his ear as she peered over his shoulder.

He had no time to reply. Banging and thumping sounded from below. Anger and determination struck his senses as people outside attempted to break in. That wedge wouldn't hold long. All it'd take was one smart person with an object thin enough to poke under the door and shove it out.

Chusho! He had no idea where to begin. Anxiety crawled through him like a swarm of those stupid island gnats.

He sat in the operator's chair, hoping for inspiration, when a grinding scrape echoed up the stairwell. Terk bounded to his feet with a curse. Those chimas weren't as dumb as he'd hoped.

"Up here!" a yell erupted from below.

Terk hissed with frustration and retrieved his bow in time to see a head appear. He fired and missed by a wide margin. He'd made his point, however. The man ducked out of sight.

"Check them for weapons!" Terk pointed his elbow at the fallen men.

While Anxi searched, Terk notched another arrow. Already, his hand ached, but battle-focus helped him press on. Someone else popped up, this time with a weapon. A spark erupted along with a bang. Bullets sprayed around him. He ducked and Anxi covered her head and cowered.

"We need weapons!" he bellowed at her.

Her eyes rounded with worry. "They didn't have any."

"Chusho!" He had to call for help, but the communications station was in view of the attackers. Anxi couldn't provide cover because the bowstring was too taut for her.

Terk loosed another arrow. "Find something! Check those cupboards. Look in the toolbox. Anything!"

If she did as told, he didn't notice as he held off the attackers. Bullets flying or not, he had to keep them from getting up here. The stairwell provided a nice chokepoint, but only for as long as he had arrows—and those were running low.

He released another arrow. A yelp erupted, followed by a sharp emotional pang. Unfortunately, the sensation didn't include the pain of death.

A slew of bullets answered. Anxi cried out. Terk risked a glance. She held her side. Blood seeped between her fingers. He sensed her hurt but so far, her lifeforce didn't seem affected.

He gritted his teeth. Pulling the bowstring sent a sharp twinge up his arm. He pressed on and loosed without aiming.

Her emotions exuded her terror and seemed to paralyze her.

"Find something or we're dead!" he screamed at her.

She shook out of her stupor and crawled to a cupboard.

"Get those bilge rats!" the captain's voice rang out.

Fear spiked through Terk's adrenaline. If that cyborg's eye had targeting capability, he'd be much better at hitting his targets. Plus he had that lightning weapon in his palm.

Terk filled his lungs, hoping to calm his rising trepidation. *Mushin, damn it.*

Taking out the captain became his priority. A few more breaths allowed him to focus his senses and bear the pain of his injured hand. His vision shifted and suddenly he saw through the captain's eyes— even the cybernetic one. He almost lost his concentration at the oddity of it but embraced the alternate view of the operations room from the stairwell.

Based on the angles, Terk calculated the captain's exact position. Back to his own vision, he stretched the bowstring. His hand throbbed and shook, but he gritted his teeth and endured. He crept forward as close to the captain's line of sight as possible without being in it. Then he prayed for a good aim.

With the hastiness of a blackbeast, he jerked into the captain's view. The chima's palm rose, glowing blue. Terk glimpsed himself. His arrow appeared dead on, so he let it go. The blue sparks in the captain's hand flittered out as the arrowhead plunged into his normal eye.

Though muted, the captain's sharp pain of death stabbed through his own emotions. Something else skewered him as he rolled out of the way. He didn't feel anything at first, but the sight of blood oozing from the flesh of his upper arm brought on a burning ache. He notched another arrow and tried to pull It back, but the searing agony was worse than his scarred hand.

"Call on the cyborgs!" someone from the stairwell yelled.

Terk's physical suffering fluttered into a debilitating fright that was almost as painful. There might be dozens of those machine-people with any number of enhanced abilities. Getting help became more imperative than ever.

A glimpse at the radio froze his blood. A ragged hole had punched through the buttons. There was no calling anyone now. They were doomed. Those men would get up the stairs eventually.

Curse his foolishness. It was better to be dead than a machine. But damn it. Going out like this demonstrated the idiotic decisions that had plagued his entire life. He almost cried at the pointlessness of it all.

The onslaught slowed as those thugs waited for reinforcements. Anxi found a first-aid kit and pressed gauze to her side. She offered some to Terk, but he ignored her. The jittering of his nerves made it too hard to move or think.

"Here they come!" someone from downstairs called out.

Since Terk sensed nothing, that only meant one thing—the cyborgs.

His world narrowed into a tiny pinprick as his entire body trembled. Those freaks wouldn't kill him in the traditional sense. They'd remake him into something else—something alive but dead—something so monstrous that even monsters would envy him.

Someone shook his shoulder. "Terk. Terk!" Anxi's voice seemed far away. "Terk, what's wrong?"

"Cyborgs," he whispered.

She slapped his cheek. "So what! They're just machines!"

He blinked. His full vision returned.

Anxi knelt before him, her emotions both fierce and afraid. "Come on! I can't use your bow without your help. Please!"

Terk snapped out of his self-pity. She was right. They were just machines—mindless robots. Nothing to be scared of.

He raised his bow. Pulling the bowstring incited a fire like none other, but he let it burn. He notched the arrow. The agony in his arm was distant enough that it didn't interfere with his focus as he took aim down the stairwell.

A bald head appeared. Then eyes. If one was cybernetic, he didn't notice. He released the arrow and watched as it flew in slow motion toward its target.

The cyborg's head snapped back and disappeared. Thumps and clanks followed as his body tumbled down the stairs.

"I found something!" Anxi held a red object. It almost looked like a gun, but its barrel was thicker than his thumb, and it didn't have a magazine.

She pulled out a red cylinder casing and tried to push it into the barrel.

Terk's trepidation fled. "Flip it," he said, hoping it worked much like another type of weapon Sensei Jeruko had taught him to use.

She turned it, but not in the way he intended. He set his bow aside and held out his hand. She tossed him the gun and the casing as though it was on fire. He flipped the barrel down and shoved it in. Hoping that was all he needed to do, he pointed down the stairwell and pulled the trigger.

Smoke and orange fire erupted and flew down in a streak. Terk shied away from the brightness. A cacophony of curses and yells broke out from below. One man bellowed in agony.

Terk's jaw dropped as he realized what this gun was for. He tossed it back to Anxi. "Shoot it out the window and into the sky!"

Her eyes widened in understanding. She stumbled to an open window with only a half-dozen more of those bullet-things. Blood soaked the bottom of her shirt and the top of her pants. She didn't emit the pain of death, but her strength dwindled.

His did as well. He only had a few arrows left and almost no ability to shoot them. If help didn't come soon, he'd die here and Anxi along with him.

16
Falling Stars

The yellow sun settled closer to the horizon. Washi Jeruko dimmed the airship's window to lessen the glare as they continued to scour the ocean. They'd altered their trajectory to make it appear as though they were headed back, but he'd drag this out for as long as possible.

He gripped the controls, wishing they were Major Whang's neck. People's lives were at stake, but that chima acted in spite rather than benevolence. He shouldn't be surprised. This seemed to be a common Toradon trait. Too many people were more concerned about exerting their power for selfish reasons.

His frustration turned to despair. Terkeshi could've left the villagers to their fate, but he ran off to help them instead. Foolish, yes, but honorable. And now he would suffer for it. The galaxy was unjust.

Heaviness weighed him down. Despite his determination to keep looking, he held no hope of finding the boy. The endless sea didn't have a single blemish. Nor did the radar pick anything up. Terkeshi was gone.

The radio crackled. "*Cormorant*, you are to return to base," Major Whang broadcasted.

Washi clenched his jaw while Michio answered. "We're on the way, Sir."

"You're off course. Head back straightaway."

Michio shot Washi a pleading look. Washi returned it with a scowl. "Fuck him." He pressed his own comm and prepped himself for a fight. "Negative, Sir. We're continuing our search. There are people out there who need us."

"Return to base at once or I'll send a squadron after you."

Washi growled, then pounded his fist on the edge of the console. "I'm not giving up!" he said to his brother.

"I'm with you," Michio replied with an earnest expression. "I don't care what the punishment is. We must help those people."

The heat building in Washi's body diminished somewhat. "If he sends a squadron, they'll shoot us out of the sky."

Michio shook his head. "That's his dishonor, not mine."

"Not mine either." Washi reopened the comm. "Major Whang. Do whatever the fuck you want. Maybe you don't care about our people, but we do and we're staying out here until we find them."

Major Whang screamed incoherently. Michio turned off the radio.

Washi blew out a puff of air. It felt good to get those words off his chest. Now if he could just find Terk and the other villagers, he'd show everyone what a small man the major was.

"Head that way," Michio said, pointing. "Since the major is sending out jets, let's make it difficult for them to catch up."

Washi turned the plane. The sun's glare lessened as it sank further. The clock ticked down in more ways than one.

"They're coming." Michio frowned at the display where three dots labeled as airships appeared.

"Damn that chima," Washi muttered.

Several minutes passed. Whang's airships drew closer. Michio tugged at his collar. Washi bit down hard enough to give him a headache.

"What's that?" Michio pointed.

Washi eased the plane to the right and squinted his eyes. "I don't see anything."

"I saw an orange light."

Doubt flittered through Washi's thoughts, but he headed in that direction anyway. A glance at the radar showed nothing, but when he looked back up, something orange sprouted on the horizon. His heart skipped a beat.

Michio jerked forward and pointed. "There it is again! Did you see it?"

"Yeah, I saw it. What was it?"

"I don't know, but it's the first thing we've seen in hours."

"It could be the sun reflecting off a whale spout."

"Impossible! For us to see it at this distance, the whale would have to be exploding." Michio's face lit up with certainty.

Washi wasn't so sure. "Anything on the radar?"

"Maybe…"

Another orange light shot upward, then fell back down like a falling star. His first thought was a missile. If someone fired a rocket, wouldn't it stay in the sky longer? And wouldn't it show up on radar? It certainly wouldn't announce itself by blazing like the sun, then drop like a rock.

"Got something." Michi's cheeks blossomed red from smiling so hard. He tilted the display toward Washi. "I think it's a ship. Someone must be trying to get our attention."

Washi remained dubious.

"It's a flare gun," a man in the cabin called out.

"A what?" Washi replied.

"A flare gun. People use it to signal for help when they can't use the radio."

Michio beamed. "It's him. It must be."

For the first time since this whole thing began, optimism infected Washi's mood. *We're coming, Terkeshi.*

17
Rescue

Sweat beaded on Terkeshi's forehead, pooled over his eyebrows, and streamed down his face. The searing pain in his shoulder as he drew the bowstring hazed his vision, but he gritted his teeth and endured. His arms shook as he nocked the arrow. Too impaired to aim, he blindly sent the projectile down the stairwell.

Luck prevailed when a man charging up the stairs pitched backward, his lifeforce shattered. Terk's relief was short-lived as two more men bounded up from behind, both firing ballistic weapons.

Terk dropped and rolled back for cover. The report of gunfire followed, piercing his eardrums. A dull pang penetrated his thigh. He had no time to wonder about it as he frantically sought for something—anything—he could use to defend himself. He grabbed a loose item and flung it at the closest attacker.

The weighted object struck the man's arm, causing him to drop his weapon. It clattered to the floor and Terk lunged for it. The cool metal in his palm offered a tremendous relief as he snatched it and fired. The man crumpled.

The other charged after Anxi, who crouched behind a chair and under a console. Terk shot him in the back, then returned his attention to the stairwell.

The heads of two more men appeared, then ducked down when Terk discharged more rounds. "I'm armed, you chimas!"

He scooted to the fallen thug and confiscated his weapon. It was a simple firearm. Signs of corrosion risked a misfire—a risk he'd take upon himself, but not Anxi. Besides, she had a more important task. "Get out there and keep firing that thing!"

"I can't!" she cried as she pressed her hands to her ears. "I'm out!"

Dread lumped in Terk's throat. He had firearms now. Pressing the trigger didn't affect his scarred palm as much, but the kickback hurt like hell. Still, aiming ballistics was easier than managing an erratic wooden projectile. He'd be out of ammo soon, though. Plus, he and Anxi were both injured.

More blasts erupted from the stairwell. Terk returned it, firing only when the opportunity presented itself. Outnumbered and outgunned, they'd reached the end of the line. No way would they survive this much longer.

"A ship!" Anxi yelled.

Terk heard her words, but they didn't register. Futile desperation coursed through every fiber of his being.

"Help is here!"

The elation in Anxi's voice caught Terk's attention. He risked a scan out the windows where someone dropped from a rappel line. His black armor, helmeted head, and high-powered rifle marked him as a soldier, but from where? Had help finally come, or did this man belong to another military group who only sought to steal from other thugs?

The soldier planted his boots on the edge of the open window and aimed his rifle inside. Terk dived for cover as blasts of phaser fire spewed down the stairwell. Yells and screams from the slavers followed.

Anxi gripped Terk's arm. "We're saved?"

He swallowed. The soldier acknowledged them with a quick head-dip and moved on. Terk sighed and nodded. "We're saved."

*****

Wind buffeted the airship, making it difficult for Washi Jeruko to keep it steady as his team rappelled down to the ship. Although he concentrated on the controls, the chatter on the radio bolstered his spirits.

"There's a firefight down here!"

"Two civilians in the control tower fending off the crew."

Michio whooped. Washi settled for a shaky laugh. One had to be Terkeshi. So far as he knew, all the other kidnapped villagers were just farmers who only wrestled livestock and shot an occasional boar.

"Man down!" a soldier said of another.

"I'm alright," came the reply.

Play-by-play radio chatter ensued as they attempted to secure the vessel. The armor his squad members wore wasn't the best, but they were better off than the shabby wear of the slavers.

"*Cormorant*!" Major Whang broadcasted from a different channel. "You have one more chance to obey orders."

"Sir!" Michio replied. "We've found our people. We're under fire and request backup!"

"Damn it, Jeruko!" Whang yelled. "Get your ass—"

Washi had no time to curse the major, nor to understand why he cut off. That radio remained silent while the chatter from the squad's channel continued.

"Tower secured. It's definitely two of our villagers here!"

Washi's heart leapt.

"I have two slavers holding out on the bow."

"Alpha team heading below deck."

The main radio clicked. "Colonel Zhou to the *Cormorant*."

Michio eagerly jabbed the comm button. "*Cormorant* here. Go ahead."

"Sitrep, now."

Michio explained in short, quick sentences. "If it's not our villagers, Sir, it's still people who need help."

"Help is on the way."

A tsunami of relief surged over Washi. Finally, someone who saw past their ego.

Events blurred from there. All the slavers, plus a few cyborgs, were either killed or captured. His squad found the prisoners and confirmed they were from the island. Twenty-one in all. The two in the tower were the only ones who needed medical attention but would be fine.

It wasn't until they'd brought the people into the *Cormorant* that Washi verified Terkeshi was one of them. Although he didn't have time to speak to the young man, the sound of his voice from the cabin lifted a tremendous weight.

*****

Washi first transported the villagers to a temporary shelter where they'd receive medical aid. His second landing of the day returned him to base. He shut down the airship, the subsequent quietness allowing him to contemplate everything.

Michio had filled him in on what Terkeshi and the others had reported. Although he still felt the young man's initial actions had been rash, he'd done well. Sneaking aboard first the submarine then the ship displayed his daring. Attempting to disable the ship showed his cunning. Leaving most of the villagers secured to protect them proved he'd had their best interest in mind. And finally, hearing how Terkeshi had infiltrated the tower demonstrated his skills.

Washi swelled with pride. All that time spent training the young man had paid off. The villagers were alive and well because of his actions.

The expected reprimand for stealing an airship never came. After making his report, Jingyu met him with a beaming smile. "The colonel is pleased with our initiative."

"What about Major Whang?"

"I saw Colonel Zhou berating him earlier. Now he's probably sulking back at headquarters."

Washi couldn't believe his luck. No, it wasn't luck. It was his stepfather. Jingyu had come through for him. He stopped and faced the man with appreciation and bowed. "Thank you, Sir."

Jingyu inclined his head. "Of course."

They parted ways, Washi with a whole new outlook that lightened his steps. He returned to the temporary medical tent and found Terkeshi pressing a bandage to his thigh while a grey-haired woman tended to his shoulder.

"You alright?" Washi asked.

"Yes, Sir. Just grazes."

"Good." Washi dithered, trying to come up with the right words to say. "You disobeyed me. I told you not to go after them."

Terkeshi looked down. "I didn't want them to get away."

"I figured as much." Washi sighed. "Good job."

Terkeshi's head shot up and his mouth hung open.

"I mean it. What you did was foolhardy, but… Well… I would've done the same in your place."

"Thank you, Sir." Terkeshi's throat bobbed.

Washi swallowed too. He had more to say, but admitting he was wrong wasn't easy. "This incident proves a few things."

A quizzical look crossed Terkeshi's brow.

"That you're more than just a farmer." A plan formed in Washi's mind. "I've been thinking. Baba Airi's not the only one who needs your help. I have a feeling that trouble is coming. These people need to learn how to defend themselves. After you finish your chores each day, I want you to train some of them."

"You expect me to turn these farmers into warriors?" Terkeshi's tone radiated incredulity.

"Not all. Just the ones you believe have potential. Teach them defense. And I want you to coordinate an escape plan for your closest neighbors. That way, if someone attacks this island, the people here can get away while you and your team guard their backs."

Terk bobbed his head. "Yes, Sir. You can count on me."

Washi clapped him on the uninjured shoulder. "I know."

*****

Terkeshi sniffled and blinked away the liquid building in his eye. He'd expected the man to give him a tongue-lashing for his foolishness. That he'd been praised meant he'd done the right thing.

He considered his new task. Forming an escape plan would be a challenge. The villagers were spread out, and some were infirm or cared for young children. Teaching defense would be even more difficult. He knew at least one person he'd train, though. Someone who had the ferocity of a blackbeast and just had their first taste of battle. Anxi was as responsible for saving those people as he was.

Despite the reason behind his new assignment, his future didn't seem so dismal. He had a purpose now—one that he was proud to fulfill.

"Oh," Washi said. "Someone wants to see you."

Terk cocked his head.

"She's in the back," Washi added.

Terk's heart swelled. His mother. He'd only seen her once since his arrival on the island, but too briefly to have any meaning. And last time, he'd met her as a failure. He could never make up for the loss of Jori, but at least he stood before her a little taller.

Before he left, Washi whispered in his ear, "Be careful. People still can't know who you are."
Terk agreed.
Who I am now is much better than who I was before.

Did you enjoy this novella? Leave a review. Authors love reviews!

How did Terkeshi go from being a prince to a farmer? Find out in the main series. If you haven't read them, search for Dragon Spawn Chronicles by Dawn Ross on Amazon.

Sign up for my newsletter by visiting my website, DawnRossAuthor.com, and get great deals!

By signing up, you'll receive a short story prequel and get access to the first few chapters of the first four books.

Connect with Dawn Ross online:
DawnRossAuthor.com
Twitter.com/DawnRossAuthor
Facebook.com/DawnRossAuthor
Goodreads.com/author/show/441861.Dawn_Ross
Patreon.com/DawnRossAuthor

Books by Dawn Ross:

<u>The Dragon Spawn Chronicles</u>

StarFire Dragons
Dragon Emperor
Dragon's Fall
Isle of Hogs (a novella)
Warrior Outcast
Orphaned Warrior
Fated Warriors
Spire Wilderness
(a novella)

Connect with Dawn Ross online:
DawnRossAuthor.com
Twitter.com/DawnRossAuthor
Facebook.com/DawnRossAuthor
Goodreads.com/author/show/441861.Dawn_Ross
Patreon.com/DawnRossAuthor

Dawn Ross

About the Author

Dawn Ross currently resides in the wonderful state of Kansas where sunflowers abound. She has also lived in the beautiful Willamette Valley of Oregon and the scenic Hill Country of Texas. Dawn completed her bachelor's degree in 2017. Although the degree is in finance, most of her electives were in fine art and creative writing. Dawn is married and has a wonderful son. Her current occupation is part time at Meals on Wheels. She is also a mom, homemaker, volunteer, wildlife artist, and a sci-fi/fantasy writer. Her first novel was written in 2001 and she's published several others since. She participates in the NaNoWriMo event every year and is a part of her local writer group.